The Lord worked in mysterious ways, there was no doubting that. Dot went to the bedside cabinet and took out her Bible. She would spend a soothing hour reading the psalms, then she'd write that note to Charlie, explaining how she'd been took funny.

She sat on the bed and opened the Bible at the marker. Her eyes danced across the words for a moment then settled at a favourite place. Clearing her throat softly, Dot started to read, her voice hushed and reverent.

'Bow down thine ear, O Lord, hear me: for I am poor and needy . . .'

By the same author

The Outsider
The Dark Side of the Sun

EastEnders Novels

Home Fires Burning
Swings and Roundabouts
Good Intentions
The Flower of Albert Square
Blind Spots
Hopes and Horizons
Growing Wild

HUGH MILLER

The Baffled Heart

EastEnders – Book 7

By arrangement with the
British Broadcasting Corporation

GRAFTON BOOKS
A Division of the Collins Publishing Group

LONDON GLASGOW
TORONTO SYDNEY AUCKLAND

Grafton Books
A Division of the Collins Publishing Group
8 Grafton Street, London W1X 3LA

A Grafton Paperback Original 1987

ISBN 0-586-07223-3

Printed and bound in Great Britain by
Collins, Glasgow

Set in Times

Prologue – 1947

Archie Blake came round the corner and paused outside a scarred old end-of-terrace house. He squared his peaked cap and touched the knot of his tie. Archie was Walford's newest Child Truancy Officer and he was about to make his eleventh call of the day. He was cold and tired and he had the feeling, more intensely than usual, that people were taking him for nothing but a mug.

He got out his notebook and checked he had the right house. 17 Carver Road. Not the fanciest address in Walford. According to the information the Colwells lived in two rooms on the first landing.

Archie knocked the door and stood back, sighing to himself. What kind of job was this for a man with his record? Just because he'd come back to civvy street with a limp, he'd been classified as semi-disabled and fobbed off with a scratchy uniform and a set of duties more suited to a half-wit. It was a poor thank-you to somebody who'd served his country for six hard, dangerous years – a man who had killed Germans *and* Japs, who had been seriously wounded three times and had twice been taken prisoner by the enemy – all in the cause of preserving a society that treated him like dirt.

An old man opened the door. Like most people when they saw Archie for the first time, he frowned. 'Yes?'

'Is Mrs Colwell in, please?'

The old man sniffed. 'What's it about?'

'It's a private matter,' Archie said. 'Is she in?'

'I couldn't say.' The old man's frown darkened as he drew his cardigan about him.

'Is there some way of finding out, then?'

The old man thought about it. 'Hang on a minute. I'll give her a shout.'

'Cheers.'

The wind was stinging Archie's ears and his bad leg was throbbing, which was enough to put up with without this faffing about. It was the same every house he called at. People were evasive and obstructive, they told him lies, some of them even swore at him. He could see himself jacking this job in if the public didn't stop giving him such a hard time.

A woman came to the door, wearing the standard frown. She was somewhere in her thirties, Archie guessed, thin with frizzy hair and a lot of make-up. 'You wanted to see me?'

'Mrs Colwell? I'm from the School Board. It's about your daughter, Dorothy . . .'

'Hey!' a woman's voice yelled from the depths of the house. 'Shut that bleedin' door, will you?'

Mrs Colwell made a face. 'You'd better come in,' she told Archie. 'Old bugger-lugs'll put the rent up if we don't do what she wants.'

They climbed the stairs to the first landing. The smell of cooking from downstairs gave way to a mustier one when Mrs Colwell opened the door to her rooms. Two small boys playing by the fireplace stopped and looked up at Archie. He smiled at them and they scowled back. Beside the table there was a cot with a baby asleep in it. A thin, gangly girl in an unseasonal print frock and scuffed slippers was stirring something on the two-burner cooker in the far corner. Archie saw her kind often. Little work-horses. They were kept away from school to look after the other kids and do the cooking while mum and dad got on with acting as if they had no children at all. She gave Archie one nervous glance then looked away.

'Sit down, if you want,' Mrs Colwell said.

'Thanks, I will.' Archie took off his cap, squeezed past the cot and perched himself on the edge of a kitchen chair. 'Well . . .' He took out his notebook and pencil. 'As I said, it's about Dorothy. She's been away from school for two and a half weeks now, and it's my job to find out why.' He glanced at the girl by the cooker. She had turned her back to him. 'Is this Dorothy?'

'Yeah, that's our Dot.' Mrs Colwell folded her arms and took up a stance by the door, as if she was going to keep Archie there until things were sorted out the way she wanted them. 'She's been sick, you see.'

'Oh.' Archie made a squiggle in his notebook. 'What's been the matter?'

'She's very chesty. Gets these attacks of wheezin', like.'

'Has she seen a doctor?'

'Oh yeah. He told me to keep her in.' Mrs Colwell's face puckered with motherly concern. 'At least a month, he said.'

Archie had heard that story more times than he could count. 'Can I have the doctor's name?'

'His name?'

'Yes, please.' The boys on the floor had moved very close to each other, staring at Archie. They didn't look as if they had been washed in days. Nothing in the place gave the impression it had been cleaned recently, for that matter. The seedy overcrowded room, the grubby kids, the put-upon older child, the mother's story – Archie knew the pattern. The army hadn't done much for his view of humanity, but in some ways this job was a bigger eye-opener.

'Well . . .' Mrs Colwell was struggling with her memory. 'It's one of those names that's hard to remember, you know?'

'Was he your usual family doctor?'

'No,' Mrs Colwell said quickly. 'He was a new man, part-timer I think. Had a foreign name.'

7

'Just give me the name of your regular doctor, then. He'll have all the details written down in Dorothy's records.' Archie read the woman's expression, seeing the caginess, the mental scramble for another way out. 'Failing that, we can arrange for a school doctor to take a look at her – just to get her properly registered sick.' Now Archie saw panic.

'She was sayin' she's feelin' a lot better.' There was a squeak at the back of Mrs Colwell's voice. 'Wasn't you, Dot?'

The girl nodded without looking up from her stirring.

'Fact is, I was thinkin' of sendin' her back to school tomorrow. An' it would save all this rigmarole, wouldn't it?'

Archie didn't feel inclined to let the woman off the hook, although now he could. All he was required to do was get the girl back at school. The other stuff – possible neglect, overcrowding, unsanitary conditions – was none of his business.

He shook his head doubtfully. 'I still have to make my report, Mrs Colwell. If a doctor told you to keep Dorothy off school, then we need a note from him. And if he said she should stay off for a month, maybe it wouldn't be wise to send her back so soon.'

'What do doctors know?' Mrs Colwell's arm shot out, one finger pointing at her daughter. 'I'm her mother, I carried her an' I've seen her through every bout of sickness since the day she was born eleven years ago. Nobody knows more about that kid than I do. An' I'm sayin' she's fit enough to go back to school.'

Archie was about to ignore the outburst and remind her about the doctor's note, then he decided to let it all drop. He was too tired and dispirited to punish the woman any longer. It wouldn't do any good, anyway. He put away his notebook and stood up. 'We'll leave it at that, then,' he said, edging past the cot again. 'But remember, Dorothy will have to be back at school tomorrow.'

'Oh, she will be.'

Archie glanced at the girl. For one instant he caught her eyes. He hadn't seen a lonelier-looking child. 'And she must attend regularly in future. She has a very poor attendance record, Mrs Colwell. She's just not getting the education she's entitled to.'

'I'll sort all that out,' Mrs Colwell promised, hurriedly opening the door. 'You can see yourself out, can't you?'

Back on the street Archie looked at his watch. There was time to make three more calls before knocking off, he estimated. Time for a few more lies, a few more depressing insights.

He checked an address in his notebook and began walking. By now he had stopped noticing the way people looked at him, their curiosity about his limp and his dark uniform. What he did notice though, constantly, was that other people always looked a lot brighter than he ever felt. There were smiles on all sides, bright chatter, people moving in currents far different from his own.

'Bloody job,' he muttered. That was the trouble, of course. His job. Sixteen months convalescing in an army hospital, then straight into this. 'Shit.' He just didn't like prying into people's lives and doing work that automatically made him a baddie. Before the war he had been a painter and decorator. Now he couldn't even stand on a ladder without hanging on. He felt a pang of regret for the old days. Painting and decorating had been good work. Happy work.

GOD BLESS THE ROYAL PAIR! said a hand-lettered card in a shop window. In a week Princess Elizabeth and Philip Mountbatten were going to be married. People were getting excited. Flags and banners were going up all over the place. Everybody was having a grand time except Archie Blake.

Things could be worse, he told himself, scarcely believing it until the image of that girl sprang into his mind. Poor skinny Dorothy Colwell. There was a word for the way she looked, with her big sad eyes, her air of bewilderment. *Dispossessed*, that was it. They used the word about the refugees, the world's lost creatures. Little Dot Colwell looked dispossessed.

God yes, Archie thought, limping along a bit faster, things could be a damned sight worse. He still had a sense of belonging somewhere. He knew who he was. Those kids, the Dots he kept seeing – what happened to them afterwards? When they grew up and went out into the world, what did they become?

1

'Be not thou envious against evil men,' Reverend Hawkins rumbled, clasping the front of the lectern. 'Neither desire to be with them.'

A woman at the front of the congregation shifted her feet anxiously and stared at her gloved hands. Further along a man was gazing at the minister and nodding.

'Their heart studieth destruction, and their lips talk of mischief.' Reverend Hawkins' eyes came up from the Bible and scanned every face in the chapel. 'Through wisdom is an house builded; and by understanding it is established.'

There was a scattering of amens as the minister closed the Bible and cleared his throat. As usual he had taken his text from the Book of Proverbs. It always provided good material for sermons that condemned the modern world, and condemnation was Reverend Hawkins' stock in trade.

'The Lord's instruction in this passage is clear enough.'

Hawkins' eyes narrowed and his tongue flicked across his lips, left to right, right to left. He had a talent for making the members of the congregation feel they were being addressed individually. He could also give them the nervous feeling that he would ask questions at any minute, just to see if they'd been paying attention.

'"Be not thou envious against evil men." That's very clear indeed. And there's a warning that even a child should be able to take – "Their hearts studieth destruction, and their lips talk of mischief." Now that is simple, fundamental wisdom and instruction. It is a pronouncement which any man or woman should find easy to observe.' Hawkins sniffed loudly, signalling a flood of his richest denunciation. 'But do we? *Do* we? In this advanced, wise, *enlightened* society, in this fifty-seventh year of the streamlined twentieth century, do we pay any heed at all to the Lord's message?'

Three rows back, Dot Colwell fought down an impulse to answer the reverend. Of course nobody took heed. You only had to look about you. You only had to look along to the end of this row. Mrs Ellis sat there with her smug face on and her fancy hat, looking like a permanent resident of the straight and narrow. But if that one's cupboard was opened, Dot knew, the noise of galloping skeletons would be deafening.

'The envy of evil men is universal,' Reverend Hawkins thundered. 'We worship dross and ordure and allow ourselves to be drawn into the clutches of diseased thinking. We condone and commit foul offences against God's grace.'

Dot was faintly annoyed that Reverend Hawkins kept saying 'we' all the time. Most people were more or less steeped in sin, she supposed, but she certainly wasn't. None of that dross and ordure for her. Whatever ordure was.

'The names of the universally worshipped are the roll-call of shame.' Hawkins shook his head with stern sadness. 'Marilyn Monroe . . .' The name, if his gulping was any guide, nearly made him sick. 'Samuel Beckett. John Osborne. Three peddlers of indecency and sacrilege. Then there is Francis Bacon, a man I'm told is a much-applauded painter, yet whose pictures are obscene, talent-less daubs. Only yesterday I saw the name of Mr Tommy Steele emblazoned across the end of a building. He typifies the new demagogues, the purveyors of chaos and mass sin – the so-called popular musicians. Worshipped by the millions, growing fat on other people's stupidity,

12

they have polluted our culture and flouted Christian ethics – *and they have done it with our full approval!*'

There were a few tentative grunts of assent.

'Their names will go down in the annals of mankind's degradation.' Hawkins' mouth twisted with disgust as he reeled off the chart-toppers. 'Lonnie Donegan, Frankie Vaughan, Johnnie Ray, Paul Anka, Dickie Valentine, Andy Williams, Guy Mitchell – mark their names well, and mark especially well the name of the arch disseminator of filth, *Elvis Presley!*'

Dot was sorry Reverend Hawkins had included Andy Williams. She quite liked him. And he'd missed out Frankie Laine, whose voice did odd things to Dot's sense of propriety. But in the main the minister was right. Music was becoming very pagan.

'"Through wisdom is an house builded; and by understanding it is established."' Hawkins braced his arms on the lectern. 'Let us examine that, and see how we may derive a measure of salvation from its meaning.'

He spent nearly fifteen minutes examining the passage. During that time a young man near Dot began to fidget. He was Greg Burton, an eighteen-year-old who only came to chapel because his father made him. After folding and unfolding his arms a few times, he let out a long, perfectly audible sigh. Dot glared at him. Greg saw her and winked. Dot looked away sharply, feeling her cheeks burn. Not even in chapel, where she took her deepest solace, was there any guarantee she'd be safe from the attentions of men.

The sermon finally ended, though not on a hopeful note. It was Reverend Hawkins' belief, stridently expressed, that humanity was so far down the road to damnation that all hope was lost. The best anybody could do was try to hang on to the few prongs of salvation that remained, and hope the tide of sin didn't wash them away.

After the service Dot went round to her mother's place, as she always did on a Sunday. Martha Colwell never seemed pleased to see her daughter, in fact she was often downright hostile. But Dot felt it was her duty to spend at least a few hours a week with her mother, now that she was a widow.

'You can put the kettle on and get some tea made before you sit down,' Martha said, leading the way into the living room-kitchen-dinette. 'Did you remember to bring some tea this time, by-the-by?'

'Yes Mum.' Dot pulled out a half-pound packet from her bag and put it on the drainer. She started unbuttoning her coat then stopped, sniffing. 'What's that funny smell in here?'

'Smell?' Martha's back stiffened and she propped her arms on her hips. It was a characteristic stance. Her husband had once said it made her look like an affronted stick insect. 'If there's a smell in here you brought it with you.'

'It's like . . .' Dot shrugged. 'I don't know.'

'It's your bloody nerves again. Makin' you imagine things.'

'Don't swear, Mum,' Dot said, trying to make the rebuke sound gentle.

'The life I've got would make a soddin' saint swear.' Martha tightened the tie-string of her wraparound apron, which she seemed to wear all the time nowadays. 'Stuck in here on me tod, never gettin' out . . .'

'You've got the kids for company.'

'Company? They've turned into a curse since their dad was taken. Rose isn't eleven yet an' already I've found dog-ends in her blazer pocket. An' the law's been round here twice in six days – once about Gerry breakin' next door's window, an' once because Tim was caught tryin' to flog kittens over by the market. God knows where he pinched them from. Told the coppers he found them.'

Martha had been moved into a council flat in 1955 when her husband Bob, a cab driver, was killed in a head-on collision with a milk tanker. Since then her personality, never noticeably sweet, had soured to the point where neighbours and her own children avoided her as much as they could.

'At least you've got a bit of room now. A lot of conveniences you never had before, too. Your own bathroom, bedroom – '

'Dot. I'm forty-four years old. I'm at an age when a woman can usually expect her life to start gettin' better. The little luxuries should be comin' along – holidays, weekend treats, a few bob in the bank. But look at me. A widow. Saddled with three kids that cause me nothin' but trouble an' eat me out of house an' home. I never get out. Nobody ever comes to see me, except you. I have to scrape along on what the National Assistance an' the Welfare'll let me have – an' you've the bloody cheek to stand there an' make out I'm in clover.'

'I wasn't sayin' that, Mum . . .'

'No, not half you wasn't.' Martha flounced across to the grubby sofa and flung herself down. That was the start of a huff. It would take a lot of wheedling and distraction to get her out of it again.

Dot filled the kettle and put it on the cooker. She wondered if maybe she should stop coming to see her mother. They always ended up having a row about something or other. But if she didn't come round nobody else would, just like Martha said.

'Did you think any more about that job I told you about?'

Martha grunted and scratched her greying frizz.

'It's an easy little job, really, Mum. Just light cleanin'.'

'I told you,' Martha said, addressing the wall above the fireplace. 'I can't go out to work. Who'd see to the kids?'

'But it'd be in school hours – '

'I'm not takin' no job!'

Dot should have known better than to suggest it. Or bring it up again. Her mother had never worked. She didn't like work, not even housework. Dot had always done that. She had practically brought up the other children, too, until she had moved into the girls' hostel, because of the overcrowding.

'Who do you think you are, anyway, handin' out suggestions an' advice like some bloody know-it-all?'

This was worse than a huff, Dot realized. She had triggered one of her mother's slanging sessions. Martha was a woman with overdeveloped resentment, and Dot was the special target, the one Martha had always seemed to prefer.

'I didn't mean to upset you, Mum.' Dot busied herself with the teacups, hoping her mother would go off the boil.

'You do it without meanin' to or tryin' to.' Martha stood up and faced Dot with folded arms and jutting chin. It was another characteristic stance, a warning that she was going to let go with both barrels. 'Miss flamin' Goody-Goody, always on hand to tell other folk what's right an' proper.'

'Mum, I never – '

'You seem to forget you was always the thickest kid in your class at school. Your teachers said you was. Thick as shit in a blanket.'

'Mum!'

'If you'd anythin' about you you'd be some help to me, real help, instead of forever tryin' to make out you know better, or you *are* better than the rest of us.'

Dot was beginning to tremble. 'I do try to help you. You know I do. But all you do is criticize. You wouldn't eat a mouthful of that dinner I made for you two Sundays ago. You wouldn't even let me help with – '

'Help?' Martha interrupted, her voice rasping. 'I was

16

talkin' about real help. You know how I've got to struggle, yet you sit on all that cash you earn an' never offer a penny to make things a bit easier. Not a brown farthing!'

Dot put down the teapot before she dropped it. 'Mum, I don't earn a lot at all. An' I've given you money. Lots of times . . .'

'An' I nearly had to beg you for it! Beggin', I was, for money that was owed me anyway!'

Dot stared at her. 'Owed? I didn't owe you it.'

Martha's face purpled with indignation. 'What about all them years I fed an' clothed an' sheltered you?' she demanded. 'Was that worth nothin'? Seems you think it was. Seems you think bein' hoity-toity an' superior gives you no obligations at all.'

'I never said I was any better than anybody else. Never.'

'Oh, is that so?'

'Yes, it is so. You've no right to say the things you say about me, Mum. I never asked for any of it.' Dot's voice was shaking, going out of control. 'I never, ever, made out I was any different to the rest of us.'

Martha came closer, wearing the threatening look she used to have before she slapped Dot on the ear. 'Every time you get somethin' new you've got to be round here paradin' it. If the boss happens to drop a compliment to you at work you can't wait to let me know. You really fancy yourself as somethin' extra special. Well I'll tell you somethin', my girl.' Martha moved so close Dot could feel her agitated breath. 'You're nothin'. *Nothin'!* All you are is a big gawky plain-jane, riddled with nerves an' religion. You'll never be anythin' else. Never! You're twenty-one an' you haven't even found yourself a bloke yet. You're not even a proper woman!'

Dot began to cry.

'That's right,' Martha grunted. 'Bubble. Bubblin' was

always your answer when anybody got you dead to rights. The truth hurts, don't it?' She reached forward and switched off the cooker. 'I don't want no tea.' She turned and walked out of the room, leaving Dot sobbing by the sink.

Late that afternoon, a young man called Charlie Cotton pressed the bellpush marked D. COLWELL by the door of the house where Dot had a bedsitter. He was good-looking in a flashy way, with chisel-shaped sideburns and Brylcreem-slicked dark hair. He was wearing his only suit and carrying a bunch of flowers.

After a minute Charlie pressed the bell again. He looked at his watch. It was bang on half-past four, the time they'd agreed. They were going to take a bus up West and walk round Hyde Park. That was the plan Charlie had put to Dot and she'd liked it. Or she'd said she did.

Charlie pressed the bell a third and fourth time, waited another minute, then shrugged. He went back down the steps, looked up at the windows, then slowly walked away.

From the window Dot saw him go. Her hankie was balled up and stuffed between her teeth to quieten her whimpering. He was carrying flowers, she noticed. Flowers. For her. She turned and threw herself on the bed, crying against the quilt.

How could she have faced him, the state she was in? He was only the second date she'd ever had. It was a meeting she had been looking forward to all week. Charlie, unlike other young men, didn't make her feel threatened. That was why she agreed to go out with him, the third time he asked her. But it would never have worked, not today, not after that business at her mother's. Dot's nerves were in too much of a state.

She wondered if her mother knew what it did to her, attacking her that way. Maybe she did know, she had always known how to reduce Dot to a trembling, sobbing, speechless wreck. A little mockery was all it took.

When she came back to the bedsitter that afternoon she sat at the window with tears streaming, thinking back over all the lonely, loveless years, right back to the time when she was three and Martha had run away and left her at that farm in Wales. It bewildered Dot that she could mean so little to her mother. She had never seemed to mean much to anyone.

But there was Charlie. He seemed to be genuinely interested in her as a person. He'd said so and it had made her blush for half an hour, just thinking about it.

Dot sat up on the bed and blew her nose. 'Got to pull yourself together,' she told herself. 'Get yourself under control.'

She stood and brushed the wrinkles from her dress. The thought of Charlie had put a spark of defiance in her. Maybe she was all the things her mother said – a plain-jane, a nothing. But she'd show her mother yet. She'd show her she *was* a real woman, with a chap of her own. A decent chap who'd respect her and shelter her.

Suddenly Dot was feeling a lot better. She knew where Charlie lived. She would go round there later and leave a note through the letterbox. Something to explain how she hadn't been feeling well enough to go out. She would square it with him.

She went to the window again. It was starting to rain. Was there a sign in that? Had providence saved her from an afternoon that might have been disastrous, a real bad start, getting soaked and all, instead of having the idyllic couple of hours she had imagined?

The Lord worked in mysterious ways, there was no doubting that. Dot went to the bedside cabinet and took out her Bible. She would spend a soothing hour reading the Psalms, then she'd write that note.

She sat on the bed and opened the Bible at the marker.

Her eyes danced across the words for a moment then settled at a favourite place. Clearing her throat softly, Dot started to read, her voice hushed and reverent.

'Bow down thine ear, O Lord, hear me: for I am poor and needy . . .'

2

'Talkin' to you,' Ricky Johnson said, 'is like pickin' up mercury with a fork.' He was leaning on the wall behind Woolworth's, talking to Charlie Cotton. Charlie was sitting on an upended milk crate moodily cleaning his nails with a penknife.

'I'm not bein' deliberately difficult,' Charlie said. 'Just sensible. If there's a risk in this, an' I'm sure there is, then I don't want to get involved. I can't afford to.'

Ricky was trying to talk Charlie into doing a job with him. He had pointed out there was good money to be made in the three-card lark. And it was safe. There was nothing much for Charlie to do except keep his eyes peeled, and for doing that he could earn himself ten quid for one day's work. So it had to be dangerous, Charlie said. That kind of money didn't come easy, not to anybody.

Ricky had pooh-poohed that and explained in detail. They would work Oxford Street and the lower end of Tottenham Court Road. Ricky would do all the real work. He was the card handler, and he was good. 'Here we go ladies an' gentlemen, try your luck at a simple game of chance.' For a table they would use a big cardboard box that was easy to abandon. The ground where they stood now was littered with them. Half a dozen or so boxes would be planted in advance, ready to be pulled into service as the game moved along.

'I've done it for years on an' off,' Ricky had said. 'It's a piece of cake.'

'An' you've got done for it on an' off,' Charlie pointed out.

'That was before I learned to work mob-handed, like they do in the States. Much, much safer that way, an' there's a hell of a lot more profit in it.'

Ricky would throw down the cards on the box and invite the mugs to find the lady. The plant, who pretended to be a passer-by and who would also be on a tenner for his day's work, would try his luck. He would find the lady. Twice. That would raise a bit of interest. Then Ricky and the plant would bet on it – two quid for starters. The plant would win again. And again. Ricky would start to look anxious.

That's when the digger would come into action. He would pretend to be another interested citizen, and he would encourage the more enthusiastic looking mugs to throw down their cash – a good, persuasive digger was worth his weight, so he would get more money than the others at the end of the day.

Around about then Ricky would start to win. But not every time, just most times. By now the fourth member of the team would be operating. He was the wedge, who got behind punters who were betting, leaning on them quite hard, inciting them to keep at it and making it difficult for them to move away. By then there would be quite a crowd round the game and team-member number five would be busy. He was the dive, the pickpocket.

The payoff was when they had what Ricky called an execution pitch. Maybe twenty people round the box, six or seven of them betting and starting to lose heavily. They would be getting anxious, betting heavy to recoup. Just at the point when Ricky gauged their suspicion would start to flare, he'd signal the digger, who would yell – 'Watch it! Coppers!' Three pairs of hands would snatch up all the money from the box and the team would dissolve into the pedestrian traffic, leaving the box behind.

'And all you have to do, Charlie my boy, is stand

22

across the road and be lookout. The hardest thing you'll need to do is whistle if you see the Law.'

Now, having thought it over, Charlie felt there had to be more to it than that. Ten quid for being lookout seemed like very high wages. What Charlie didn't take into account, because he didn't have the savvy, was that someone who whistled always attracted attention to himself – the attention of the police as much as anyone. Policemen knew a lookout when they heard one. Although the other members of the team could vanish into the crowds, the lookout would be easy to nail. And lookouts always got a hard time from the Law.

'There's safety in numbers,' Ricky reminded Charlie. He held up the fingers of one hand and gave them names. 'The Dealer, the Digger, the Wedge, the Dive an' the Whistle. All for one an' one for all. Money for jam.'

Ricky Johnson was thirty-five. He was tall and thin with a waxy, expressionless face that could conceal anything, except the fact that he was some kind of criminal. Ricky had moved to Walford at the age of thirty-one after completing his fourth prison term – for posing as a rent collector. He made the move because he had become too much of a focus for police attention on his home turf in Stepney. Any time a crime was committed that bore even the vaguest marks of his style, Ricky was pulled in. And he couldn't get up to any serious villainy any more, anyway, because he was always being watched. In Walford he had so far avoided any serious scrapes with the police, although nobody regarded him as anything like an upright citizen.

'The thing is,' Charlie said, 'I don't want any more marks on my record . . .'

Ricky groaned. 'You've not been listenin' to me, have you? Christ, do you think *I* want to get picked up again? I wouldn't get into this if I didn't know it was a safe number.' He looked about him, then reached into his inside pocket and pulled out a wad of fivers. He shook it under Charlie's nose. 'That's one third of last week's haul. A third, Charlie. An' we only worked a total of maybe an hour to get it. Good wages, good workin' conditions. We work ten minutes to a pitch, take an hour off so the faces move on, then do another ten minutes and so forth until the pubs open.' He put the money away again. 'You'll never get a better offer.'

'How come you need a new lookout this week?'

'Graham's workin' with Mossie right through the weekend. Somethin' to do with a shipment of brass ornaments. He's a mug, that Graham. Always gettin' into pony deals when he could be makin' his money the easy way. He's a good lookout, mind you. An' so are you. That's why I'm askin' you. We've worked together in the past. I trust you.'

Charlie had never done lookout in daylight before. The last time he had stood in a phone box opposite a chemist's shop, pretending to make a call while Ricky and another man broke into the shop through the side door and loaded up a van with drugs. The other man, it turned out, worked for a burglar alarm company. Ricky certainly had connections, even if they never seemed to last.

'Come on, mate, what do you say? I don't want to go puttin' my trust in some stranger. I'd rather have you along. An' I know you could use the moolah.'

That was true enough. Charlie had been kicked out of his job three weeks ago for bad time-keeping. He was behind with his rent, and now he was taking Dot out regularly his expenses were rocketing. It was a blessing she preferred coffee bars to pubs.

'Well . . .' He looked at Ricky, trying to imagine he was placing himself in safe hands. 'I suppose it's OK. Yeah, right, I'll do it.'

'That's my man.' Ricky slapped Charlie's shoulder.

'Now that's settled an' we don't have to worry about bein' earwigged, we can go an' have a pint, eh?'

'Good idea.' Charlie followed Ricky across the open ground to the pavement.

'If you like the work,' Ricky said, 'the job's yours on a regular basis.'

'Yeah, well. I'd have to think about that.'

Ricky grinned. 'You're a cautious bugger, Charlie. I'll say that for you.'

Charlie shrugged. He was wondering what Dot would think if she ever found out what he had just agreed to do. He wondered what she would think if she knew he already had a record. Charlie didn't want Dot to know any of it. He wanted her to go on believing he was a nice, considerate, gentlemanly bloke, decent and honest. That was what he wanted to be, anyway.

It was tea break at Carter's Confectionery. The three girls on first turn were huddled in the partitioned corner of the packing bay that served as kitchen and rest room. Effie, a Scots girl with open-faced good looks and a spectacular bust, was sitting on the only chair because she had got there first. The other two, Frankie and Dot, had to content themselves with a lean on the sink.

Tea breaks were awkward occasions lately, ever since it had become general knowledge that Effie was having an affair with the factory manager, Mr Truscott. Frankie didn't really hold it against Effie, since she was a pretty girl herself and knew the political advantages of putting herself about in the right quarters. But Dot had tried, unsuccessfully, to have the tea-break roster changed. It offended her to have to spend her break in such close contact with a girl who would get up to Lord-knows-what with a married man. Just before the tea bell went Dot and Frankie, who worked side by side on caramel packaging, had been discussing the difficulty of staying decent in a society that placed so much store by unseemly behaviour. It had been a fairly one-sided discussion, since Frankie would rather have talked about films or music. With somebody else.

Now, waggling her head over her steaming mug of milky tea, Dot seemed keen to keep the discussion going. 'Self-respect isn't automatically yours for good,' she said. 'You have to earn it every day.'

'I suppose so,' Frankie said. She had kept trying to ground the topic by contributing nothing, but that didn't lower Dot's enthusiasm. It did just the opposite – it gave her the floor to herself.

'It's a struggle keeping your good name,' Dot sighed.

Effie looked up brightly. 'I used to know this fella, he was a school teacher, and he was always coming out with these dead clever remarks. He said self-respect's nothing more than being sure that nobody suspects you yet.'

Dot stared at her. 'I'd say it's a *lot* more than that.'

'What is it, then?'

'Well, it's . . .' Dot waved her hand and waggled her head again. 'It's knowing, in yourself that is, that you're . . . that you're, well, decent.'

Effie nodded. 'So what's decent?'

Dot took a panicky gulp of tea. 'It's obvious, isn't it?' She looked sharply at Frankie, as if she deserved some support. Dot's moral code came from tracts and sermons and a nervous wariness of pleasure. She wasn't good with questions that required her to explain her ethics. 'Being decent is being wholesome, pure . . .'

'Like a fresh-baked loaf.'

It occurred to Dot that she was being baited. Other girls had said Effie was very good at teasing people and mocking them if she wanted to. She had a sharp tongue, the forewoman had said. Dot looked at her sitting there, smiling, looking as innocent as a shampoo advert. Somebody like Reverend Hawkins would have tackled her squarely. He would have faced her with her wickedness. But Dot didn't feel up to that.

'I'll tell you what,' Effie said. 'All this twaddle about self-respect is just rubbish, if you ask me.'

'How can you say that?' Dot demanded. 'Where would the world be without decency and moral standards? Things are bad enough as they are, but I can't imagine what they'd be like if we all just decided that human decency was rubbish.'

Effie was shaking her head. 'What I'm saying is, self-respect and *decency* are just notions, aren't they?'

'No, they're not,' Dot snapped, 'since you ask.'

'Really? Listen. A lot of real old monsters reckon they've a right to respect themselves and be respected by other people just because they don't allow themselves any pleasures. They reckon you can be grumpy, mean, vicious, cruel even, but as long as you don't smoke or drink or have it off with blokes, you're a perfectly decent person.'

'If you don't mind,' Dot squeaked, banging down her mug, 'I'd rather you didn't indulge in filthy talk near me.'

Effie stared at her, then at Frankie. 'What's she on about?'

Frankie realized she was being called upon to take sides. So she did. 'You mentioned having it off, Effie. That's a dirty thing to say, in Dot's book.'

'It must be a hell of a big book, then.'

'She gets a bit touchy about words like "tit" and "bum", too,' Frankie said, glad she had finally aired her annoyance with Dot's prudery. 'She even blushes if she finds out a bloke's called Dick.'

Dot launched herself away from the sink with both hands and hurried out into the bay. She went straight to the toilet and bolted herself in. She would stay there, her back pressed to the door, until her nerves calmed. She had found it was the only thing to do when something at

27

work upset her as badly as she was now. In this state she couldn't defend herself. She couldn't do *anything*.

Life was so harsh. There were times when she felt like some fragile thing being tossed about in churning water with rocks all around, ready to smash her. Why were people so cruel, so wicked?

She forced her mind towards calm, soothing things. She thought of the chapel. She thought of Charlie. Dear Charlie. He wasn't like the rest of them. He was as sensitive as she was, sensitive and good. But she didn't think he was as vulnerable as she was. He was strong. He could shelter her.

'Charlie,' she whispered. She wished it was Saturday and she could see him again. That seemed such a long time away. If only he could be there with her, right now, consoling her. Dot sighed, then felt herself reddening at the sudden thought of him standing beside her, locked in the ladies' loo.

One drink had led to another and another. Time had passed with unbelievable speed as the talk rambled over this and that and settled on women.

'Time for one more,' Ricky said, rising and taking their empty glasses to the bar.

'Just a half for me.' Charlie stubbed out his cigarette and sat back with his head against the leather padding. The pub was dark, even though the sun was shining outside. Charlie liked drinking in dark places. He didn't even like the door being left open. The darker and gloomier the better. He wondered if that had something to do with his own shadowy nature. There were things about himself he wouldn't ever be able to tell anybody, even if his life depended on it.

He hoped Ricky wouldn't go on about Dot again when he got back from the bar. He was too nosey when it came to other people's love lives. Not that Charlie had a love life to talk of. But Ricky's curiosity made him feel obliged to bend the facts, because the bare-bones truth was too private.

'Aw, Ricky, I said a half.'

'Get it down you,' Ricky said, setting the pint in front of Charlie. 'There's always room for one more.'

Charlie picked up the glass and stared at it sullenly. 'Cheers,' he grunted, and took a swallow.

'All the best.' Ricky gulped down a third of his pint and smacked his lips. 'So,' he said, putting the glass down again. 'You've been goin' steady with this one for two months. That's a long time for you. Must be serious.'

'We just get on well together.' That was no lie. But the full truth was that Dot got on well with the front Charlie put up. She didn't know him at all. 'We've got things in common.'

Ricky winked. 'I can guess what.'

'It's not all down to that,' Charlie said. None of it was down to *that*.

'How come we never get to see her? Frightened somebody'll pinch her?'

'You asked me that already. I told you, we don't go out much, an' when we do it's never to pubs.'

'I knew a bird like that once. Would never go in a pub. But I didn't mind. On the nights I went round to her place I spent two an' three hours, on average, workin' up a thirst for the next night.' Ricky grinned, showing snaggly teeth. 'Thirstiest work I know.'

'Yeah, right.' Charlie hadn't laid a hand on Dot. She wouldn't let him. In fact the one time he had tried she had reacted so violently he had apologized and promised it would never happen again. His mates would have wondered why he didn't ditch her if they'd known things were that way. 'What about you an' Sandra? Still hittin' it off?'

'Sort of,' Ricky said. Sandra was a barmaid from the

Queen Victoria down at Albert Square. She was big and noisy and vulgar, and she suited Ricky perfectly. 'A bit demandin', though, an' I don't just mean in bed. She behaves like I'd a duty towards her, know what I mean? "Where was you last night?" an' "There's me stuck at home while you're out with the lads." All that kind of thing. I don't know, I might give Sandra the heave. I'll wait until somethin' else is in sight, though. Don't jump off the raft you're on until you've built another one alongside, right?'

Charlie nodded, not sure if he agreed or not. Dot had changed his views on a lot of things. She'd changed his view of himself, for a start.

The barman called time. Ricky finished his pint and the half that Charlie couldn't manage. When they went out they stood blinking in the sunshine, lighting cigarettes.

'Reckon I'll go over the bettin' shop,' Ricky said. 'Comin'?'

'Nah. I've one or two things to do.'

'Right. Then I'll see you Saturday for our little jaunt up West. OK?'

Charlie nodded. 'See you.' He watched Ricky saunter off towards the High Street, then turned and began walking in the opposite direction.

Something had come to him while he was talking in the pub. It was when Ricky had talked about having a duty towards Sandra. It dawned on Charlie how much he wanted to have a duty towards Dot, a real and binding duty, something he must honour. Everything about the girl put that longing for service in him, a desire to be of use to her and to make her happy.

That was definitely odd, for him. One of the things about himself he would never tell anybody was that he had no feelings for other people. He had no capacity for real friendship, and certainly none for love. He hadn't even loved his mother, or any of his girlfriends before Dot. He hadn't hated them either. He just felt nothing. Feelings had to be faked.

In Dot he had found something extraordinary. It couldn't be explained by her looks, which were quite ordinary, or her nature, which was nervous and with-drawn. But the moment Charlie had seen her, sitting in a milk bar with one of the girls she worked with, he had known there was a special bond, or the capacity for one. For the first time he felt something powerful for a girl. And having found she wasn't easy, he was drawn to her even more strongly.

It came back to him as he crossed the street, heading for a newsagent's; that need for a duty, a bounden duty. That was it, he decided. That was the clincher. Dot made him feel good, she made him want to be a better person. She even made him want to serve her and protect her. This coming Saturday night, he would ask her to marry him.

The decision made him feel dizzy. He stopped by the newsagent's window. He thought it over. It still seemed right. They were the right age, too. She was twenty-one, he was twenty-two. A good age to set out to build a life together. A long, happy married life.

Smiling to himself, he went into the shop and straight across to the rows of magazines. From the top row, the row that concerned him, naked and half-naked women smiled and leered and pouted down at him. He hesitated and finally took down one called *Slinky Sluts*. He leafed through it for a minute and decided it was the one for him. He went to the counter and handed over his money.

Going out he reflected that Dot wouldn't understand his taste for the kind of thing rolled up under his arm. That didn't matter, for she would never find out. The day would come when she would make him a better bloke. A man she would be proud of. In the meantime he was doing his best. Part of doing his best was staying faithful to Dot. But a man was only human. He had to do *something*.

3

It rained early on Saturday, but by the time the team were assembled in the gardens at Soho Square the clouds had cleared and the sun was shining. Ricky Johnson and his digger, Bert Brennan, a man as broad as he was long, had already planted cartons in alleys along Oxford Street and Tottenham Court Road. With his head jerking from side to side, like a soldier watching for snipers, Ricky gave his troops a brief pep talk.

'We've got to remember it's all to do with pace,' he told them. 'Once the game's underway there's got to be no slackin'. No slowin' up. I'll keep the spiel goin' fast an' furious an' I expect every one of you to back me.' He nodded to a slab-faced boy called Chip, who was the pickpocket. 'Take maximum advantage. When the pitch starts gettin' hot their attention's fixed on the cards. You could steal their trousers if you wanted. Get all you can an' keep movin'.'

'I know me stuff,' Chip assured him, with some professional haughtiness. 'Don't worry about me.'

'An' you, Charlie. Even though you're not inside the action, you've got to feel like you are. Make yourself believe your neck's on the block, that you're as much a target for the cops as we are. That'll keep you sharp, alert.'

'Your neck *will* be on the block if the scuffers nab us,' Bert Brennan warned Charlie. 'Our block, that is.'

'Charlie's a good lad,' Ricky said. 'I've worked with him. He wouldn't be here if I couldn't trust him to do the job.' He looked at his watch. 'Right. It's time we were movin'. First pitch in five minutes, outside Bourne an' Hollingsworth's.'

They split up, leaving the gardens by three different gates. Charlie took the exit that led on to Sutton Row, walked along to the end and turned left out on to Charing Cross Road. The streets were busy. Plenty of tourists, strangers. Charlie felt nicely anonymous. He had expected to feel more nervous. There was a tingle of anticipation, certainly, the kind that was always there when he embarked on something new. But that was all. The job, after all, was a doddle.

Underlying the self-assurance there was real nervousness, though. It was a jumpy feeling, still far from the surface but detectable, all the same. Tonight was the big night. Tonight he would pop the question, as they said. He would put the major, earth-shaking proposition to Dot. He had tried rehearsing what he would say, but had finally given up, knowing it would be best to wait and judge Dot's mood before deciding on his approach. As he took the left turn on to Oxford Street he pushed tonight's business as far from his mind as he could. The job was on, and he was being paid enough to give it all his attention.

He took up his stance on a street corner opposite Bourne and Hollingsworth's. From there his warning whistle, if one was needed, could easily be heard by the team. It was also an ideal lookout point; he could see both ways along Oxford Street and down behind him into Soho.

After a minute he saw Ricky appear, carrying a big cardboard box. He was walking casually, his face bland as ever, eyes narrowed as he nonchalantly looked fore and aft, satisfying himself the coast was clear. He glanced across the road to make sure Charlie was there, then he dropped the box.

Charlie couldn't hear what Ricky was saying, but

straight away he began addressing the passers-by as he threw his three cards down on the box, turning them over and flipping them face up again. Charlie spotted the plant, Eggo Kelly, so-called because of his large, oval, balding head. Together with a handful of other pedestrians he had stopped to watch Ricky. Further along the street Bert Brennan was waddling into view. Chip, the pickpocket, was coming from the other direction. Everything was falling into place. Charlie stopped watching the action and began scanning the immediate vicinity, which was what he was being paid for.

Glancing to the right he saw a beautiful red-and-white car approaching, its chrome and paintwork gleaming. It was a Ford Zephyr convertible, a brand new one by the look of it. Charlie fancied owning a car like that. Maybe he would, one day. Maybe when he had knocked himself into shape – which would be easy, because he would have somebody to do it *for* – he could find the kind of job that would pay the kind of money a man needed for luxuries like that. He could always save, anyway. That was something else he wanted to try. Get some money in the bank, set up himself and his wife with a cushion, a bit of security. God, he hoped she would marry him. They could do such things together, things he could never do on his own, not without the incentive of – *Get your mind back on the job!*

He shook himself, looking around sharply for helmets. Daydreaming was the last thing anybody should do on lookout. It was worse than being short sighted. He peered right towards St Giles Circus, left along both sides of the street as far as he could see, then down the street behind him. Nothing. Not a rozzer to be seen. Charlie smiled to himself, thinking it was nice to know they were sometimes never around when you didn't need them.

He looked across at the action. There was a sizeable crowd round the game now. Ricky was pulling them in, all right. It was Charlie's opinion that if Ricky straightened himself out, he could make a real success of something that didn't carry the risks of what he usually did for a living. He had energy, plenty of flash, imagination. Charlie would bet that most of the people riding by in their big cars, looking all fat and sleek and dripping with gelt, didn't have half Ricky's talent. Maybe it was what a lot of people round Walford said – it's not what you know that gets you on top, it's where you come from. Charlie hoped that wasn't true. He didn't want to be a flop. He wanted . . .

He shook himself again. Maybe it was the heat of the sun that was doing it, making him drift off when he should be sharp as a razor. He looked both ways, then behind. Still nothing. Fine. Everything was fine.

The crowd around the game was even bigger now. He could hear Bert Brennan's voice, raised excitedly, goading some poor mug into laying out more of his cash. It was like being at a play. All that acting, all that fakery.

Charlie stiffened. Something was wrong. There had been a loud thump, like a drum being struck. Now he could see it was the cardboard box, being kicked out through the crowd and into the gutter. The man kicking it was big and broad, a mean-faced individual in an electric-blue mohair suit. As the crowd parted and began dissolving Charlie saw Ricky and Eggo. They were both being held by men very much like the one reducing the box to tatters. Ricky's arm was twisted up his back and he was yelling with pain. Eggo was on his knees, held there by a beefy hand clamped round the back and sides of his neck.

'Bloody hell.' Charlie decided it was time to shift. He didn't know what the score was and he didn't want to know. He turned about, deciding to vanish into Soho. He took five strides and a man stepped into his path. Charlie tried to walk round him. The man grabbed Charlie's lapel.

'Gentleman wants a word with you, son.'

Charlie gulped. 'What?'

'Get in the motor.'

There was a black Hillman Minx by the kerb, its engine running. The back door was open. The man pushed Charlie towards it.

'What's this all about?'

'Just get in.'

Charlie slid into the back seat. His mind was spinning, heart thudding. The man came in behind him. The door was banged shut. A foreign-looking character behind the wheel rammed the accelerator and took them tearing away into the heart of Soho.

Charlie glanced at the man beside him. He looked like a well-dressed ape. He was staring straight ahead, face impassive, a hand bunched lightly on each knee. Anxious as he was to know what was happening, Charlie didn't feel up to asking again. He pushed himself into the corner, feeling a queasy shifting in his bowels.

The ride lasted less than three minutes. The car stopped outside a building on Dean Street.

'Out,' the man said.

Charlie fumbled with the door handle, trying to figure it out.

'Push it down.'

Charlie did and the door swung open. He thought of running, but only for a second. He didn't reckon he had the strength or co-ordination to carry him a couple of yards.

The man came round the back of the car and pointed at a recessed doorway with a passage beyond. 'In there.'

They went along the passage and up two flights of stone steps. The man kept behind Charlie all the way, his heels clopping, dictating their pace. On the second landing there was a blue-painted metal door. The man banged it twice with the side of his fist. They waited as a lock was undone. Charlie could hear the blood pounding in his ears.

The door was opened by another ape look-alike. It began to seem the world was populated by big men in suits, with the exception of Charlie, five-eight in a windcheater and corduroys.

'In you go, Sunshine.'

The place looked like a club. As Charlie was guided right and through an archway he realized it *was* a club. There was flock wallpaper, deep carpet and dim coloured lights. He registered some white-covered tables, a bar and a lot of tall-stemmed artificial plants. He glanced over his shoulder. The man who let them in had joined the other one. Charlie swallowed and looked away.

He was taken into a bare room at the back of the club. There was no wall decoration, no floor covering. Only a chair and a small square table. There were no windows and the light came from a metal-shaded bulb on the ceiling.

'Wait there.'

The door shut and Charlie was alone. After a minute he began to feel worse than he had in the car. *What in the name of Christ is going on?* He wondered if it would be all right for him to sit down. His knees were shaking. It would have helped if there was even something to hold on to. He stepped to the middle of the room and put his hands on the back of the chair, letting his weight sag against his stiffened arms.

'God, Jesus . . .' he groaned.

The door burst open, making him jump back. The men he had seen on Oxford Street came in, pushing Ricky and Eggo in front of them. Eggo's nose was bleeding.

Ricky was even paler than usual and he looked badly scared.

'Against the wall, all three of you,' one of the men ordered.

As Charlie obeyed he caught Ricky's glance. He was bewildered too. Eggo just looked numb.

They stood with their backs to the wall for over a minute, trying not to meet the eyes of the two men, who stood by the table, staring at them. Then another man came in and the two by the table stepped back deferentially.

'Thank you, Angus. Thank you, Victor.'

The man sat down, carefully drawing back the knees of his trousers to prevent them creasing. He didn't look like the others. His fair hair was expensively clipped and he had the lightly-tanned face of an actor, Charlie thought, or maybe a politician. It was hard to guess his age. Somewhere in the forties, but youthful with it. His suit wasn't as flash as the others. It was dark brown, with a very thin stripe, and his tie was the same colour. He would have looked important anywhere.

'So. It's, ah, Mr Johnson, isn't it?' The man tilted his head, waiting for Ricky to look at him.

'Yeah,' Ricky croaked. 'Ricky Johnson.'

'And my name's Bridges. *Mister* Bridges.'

Ricky was moistening his palate, making a sound like wet rubber flapping. 'What's goin' on, Guv?' It came out more like a plea than a question. 'What're we here for?'

'Because you've been bad boys.' Bridges winced, as if the fact pained him. 'Trespassing's an offence. You were, ah, trading on my patch.'

'Christ, Guv, I didn't know we was – '

'You were warned, over a month ago. A man spoke to you, if you'll remember, when you were in the Horse Shoe on Tottenham Court Road, spending your ill-gotten gains.'

Ricky's eyes went distant. Charlie began to feel very panicky. This was some turn-up. He was only shut in a room in Soho on the wrong end of the Mob. Nothing this bad had ever happened to him before. Nothing so fraught with pain. With agony. He'd heard about Bridges. There were stories about him, horror stories, that had spread a lot further than Walford. And this was to have been a simple job, a doddle. At that moment Charlie had it in him, at least in spirit, to kill Ricky Johnson.

'I didn't know about no warnin',' Eggo said.

Bridges shrugged. 'Mr Johnson must have forgotten to tell you.' He looked at Ricky again. 'Last week you were back, chancing your arm again. My people were busy on other matters, so you were able to carry on. But your visit didn't go unnoticed. Today we were waiting for you. We were pretty sure you'd show up. You look the greedy sort.'

'That guy,' Ricky said, 'the one in the pub. I didn't take him seriously. I was sure he was some joker . . .'

'Correction,' Bridges said. 'You thought things would, ah, blow over.'

'He didn't mention your name, Guv. If he had, I'd have listened. Straight I would.' Ricky took a step forward, one hand raised in supplication. 'I *swear* I won't come back again, on my mother's – '

His voice cut off with a gulp as one of the big men shoved him back against the wall.

'I know you won't be back,' Bridges said calmly. 'No need for promises.' He stood up. 'You other two – I'd advise you to have no more to do with Mr Johnson. He doesn't operate in a way that takes your safety into account. He's something of a chancer. Chancers are bad news.'

He moved across the room and stopped in front of Ricky. 'Today, three other chancers have been misbehaving on my patch. One of them doesn't know the territory's mine. The others do. Pitching in Soho, Oxford Street, Charing Cross Road and Leicester Square is *verboten* to outsiders. The afore-mentioned chancers will remember that. You'll bear it in mind too, Mr Johnson. Won't you?'

'Definitely,' Ricky said.

Bridges nodded and walked to the door. He opened it. 'You'll get off with a warning, this time.' Relief flooded through Charlie and across Ricky's face until Bridges added, 'A physical warning.' He went out, closing the door.

The two men advanced.

'Please,' Ricky gurgled. Listen . . .'

Charlie pressed back, trying to make himself part of the wall. He didn't look when Ricky howled. He didn't want to see. Sweating, shaking, he clenched his teeth. His whole being was a throbbing prayer for mercy. One of the men stepped close to him. Charlie stared into his face, seeing terrible calm. He heard Ricky howl again. The man in front of Charlie was motionless, just looking at him. Then he seemed to jerk, a split second before Charlie screamed, convinced his testicles had caught fire.

Dot waited in the coffee house for an hour. Minute by minute her fear and uncertainty had mounted. Charlie was never late. Never. Something might have happened to him. That was a bad enough thought. Or he had decided not to see her again, which was miles worse.

After three coffees she left and walked slowly back home. She shouldn't have drunk so much, she thought. It had made her jumpier than she would have been. Something to do with caffeine, she'd been told. She was trembling, and she felt a terrible apprehension, as if at any minute she would learn some awful truth.

As she rounded the corner and approached the house where she lived, she saw someone leaning on the railings outside. Not a prowler, Dot hoped. *Please God don't let it be a prowler or a molester . . .*

As she came closer her heart suddenly lurched. It was Charlie! Coming closer still she realized there was something terribly wrong with him. He was hunched over, clutching his chest, breathing in grunts.

'Charlie?'

He turned his head and looked at her.

'Oh my good Lord!' Dot rushed forward. Charlie's face was bruised and swollen. His lip was split and there was blood on his chin. 'What happened to you?' Her hands fluttered about his face, powerless to do anything. 'Charlie!'

'I . . .' He groaned and clutched his chest tighter. 'I got jumped.'

'Oh that's disgraceful!' Dot peered closely at his face. 'Should I get you to a doctor?'

'No,' Charlie grunted. 'I'll be all right.'

'You certainly don't look all right. You look terrible. Let me get you round to – '

'Dot.' Charlie was looking at her with wide, beseeching eyes.

'You can't be left like this, Charlie. You've got to get help.'

'Dot, listen.'

'What?'

Charlie took a deep, careful breath. His eyes seemed to get wider. 'Will you marry me?'

Dot blinked. 'Pardon?'

'I said, will you marry me?' From the look of him it was the most important thing in the world, in spite of his injuries.

'Well, I don't – I mean I . . .' Dot stood gazing at Charlie's broken face. All of this was dizzying, bewildering. She was sure she'd have to sit down on the step.

4

After a week of soul-searching, of asking herself dozens of circular questions, Dot went to see Reverend Hawkins. She had never been in his house before. She found the place something of a surprise. A disappointment, in fact.

She had always assumed, because he was a minister of religion, that the reverend's home would *look* the part, it would mirror its owner's fierce adherence to the faith, his dedication. She had expected something like an extension of the chapel, with a few domestic touches. But she found no such thing. Reverend Hawkins' wife, Estelle, had made a home that reflected her own bland personality and took no account of her husband's character or calling. Dot thought it looked a bit like the furniture corner in those places where you could buy household goods with credit vouchers.

'Well now, this is a surprise.' Hawkins showed Dot into the living room, a place smelling of pine and lavender, pink-and-brown carpeted, with a couch and wooden-armed chairs that nearly matched the floor covering. Estelle shuffled off to the kitchen to make a pot of tea. 'Do sit down, Dorothy.'

'Thank you, Reverend.' Dot noticed he was wearing slippers made from pale-brown stuff resembling the material they used to make teddy bears. They looked odd with his clerical grey suit and dog collar. 'I hope I'm not disturbin' you.'

'I'm always here when my congregation need me,' Hawkins said. 'There's no trouble, I hope?'

'No.' Dot composed her hands on her lap. 'Well yes. But not trouble, actually . . .'

'Take your time, Dorothy. Tell me about it calmly.'
Hawkins lowered himself into the chair opposite.

'It's this chap I know . . .' Dot's eyes, darting about,
settled on a brass coal scuttle in the tiled hearth. It looked
like brass, although it was just a shade too shiny to be the
real thing, she thought – but it was something solid to
look at while she explained. 'I've been seein' him, as it
happens. Walkin' out with him, like. Quite a while now.'

Hawkins' face grew a little stern. 'What sort is he? Is
he in the congregation?'

'He's nice, really nice,' Dot said, 'but no, he doesn't
come to chapel.' She moistened her lips. 'Not that he's
an atheist or anythin' like that. He's just like a lot of
people are – a believer, but never been disciplined to go
to church regularly. He's a year older than me an' his
name's Charlie Cotton. About a week ago things went
serious between us.' Her eyes flickered and she shifted
in her chair. 'I'm sorry, Reverend, it's just that I get
embarrassed, tryin' to talk about it . . .'

Hawkins nodded, frowning as he analysed the meagre
information. When he spoke his voice was much lower
than before. 'You can talk to me frankly about this,
Dorothy. Hold nothing back.'

'Well, Charlie asked me to marry him. That's the whole
up an' down of it.'

Hawkins frowned.

'So.' Dot shrugged and then she giggled, although she
hadn't meant to. 'That's what I've come about.'

Hawkins pursed his mouth testily. 'What?'

'About marryin' Charlie. I can't make up my mind
about it. It's such a big step . . .'

'Indeed it is.' Reverend Hawkins stood up again, looking faintly disappointed. He made the motions of button-
ing his jacket, but stopped short of actually putting the
button through the button hole. He stroked his chin,
grunted, then looked at Dot with his head lowered, so

that his eyes observed her through the fringe of his brows. 'There are a few things you must ask yourself.'

'I've been doin' that all week. Askin' myself questions, not comin' up with any answers.'

'What have you been asking yourself?'

'Oh, lots of things, Reverend.' Dot let her gaze wander around the room. She saw a picture of a Scottie with a tartan coat on, a plaster boy on the sideboard lowering cherries into his gaping mouth, an empty glass fruit bowl on a spindly table. 'What it all boils down to, you see – I'm sure I won't ever like anybody more than I like Charlie, but I get the feelin' this is too soon to get married, too early-on, you know? Then, just when I think that, I think, well no, because we should get our marriage started as soon as possible so we can have our best years together, be settled-down an' sorted-out while we're young . . .'

'So what you have brought me,' Hawkins said, 'is your uncertainty.'

'I suppose so, yes.'

'And I say again, you must ask yourself a few things – fundamental things, questions that touch on your duties towards God's commandments, as well as towards a husband.'

Dot nodded, wishing she had come to the minister sooner. These were the tones and turns of speech that made her feel better, more sure of herself. Since the day and hour she had been introduced to the chapel Sunday School by a friend, she had drawn tremendous solace and strength from religion. Hawkins' words were like balm on her soul.

'First, Dorothy, ask yourself if you truly love this man. Your feelings for him – are they feelings that will last? Or are you being lured into false love, hollow love, by the goadings of the flesh?'

Dot thought about that for a moment. She didn't

recall any particularly fleshy feelings where Charlie was concerned. Where anybody was concerned, for that matter. She just knew she liked being with him. He made her feel wanted. And safe.

'You must also ask yourself,' Hawkins went on, 'if you feel a true bond of loyalty to the man, a bond that can withstand the temptations which will beset you as the years pass.' His eyebrows came very close together. 'This is a wicked world, Dorothy. Temptation has to be taken into account. It exists on all sides.'

Dot didn't have to think about that one. 'I wouldn't ever be tempted to stray, Reverend,' she said, blushing and twiddling her fingers. 'And what I feel for Charlie is real, not false. I'm sure of that.' Why hadn't she asked herself questions like these before? They were down-to-earth, they were basic. All that wondering about it being too soon and so on – that hardly mattered. The thing that counted was the nature of their need for each other. If that could be examined and found to be sound, then everything was in order. Good old Reverend Hawkins, Dot thought. He could always get to the core of things.

'And what about this young man, Dorothy? Can he be relied upon? Is he steadfast?'

That was something she had asked herself. It had been early in their relationship, at a time when Charlie let it drop that he'd known quite a few other girls. Dot had wondered if it was in his nature to flit from girl to girl and never go for solid attachments. She had heard of chaps like that, she even believed she had known a few – neighbours' sons and husbands, men with a reputation for being fickle and untrustworthy. A few of the girls at work had boyfriends who were the same. As the weeks passed Dot had made her comparisons, though, and she had come to the conclusion that Charlie was as upright and loyal as he insisted he was.

'I think,' she told Hawkins, 'that Charlie is as honest

and good a young man as I've ever met. He's respectful to me, he's considerate and he says he wants me to be his wife.' Provoking another blush, she added, 'I've never been happier in the company of anyone.'

Hawkins didn't look convinced. 'Marriage is an enormous step. You say it's only been a week since he asked you?'

Dot nodded. 'Eight days, to be precise.'

'Too early yet to make a decision, then. Dwell on the questions long and carefully. Examine the smallest doubt. Only then . . .'

The door opened and Estelle Hawkins brought in the tea on a plastic tray. She was a mousy woman with eyes as moist as a spaniel's. She looked at Dot as she set the tray on the table. It was the same look she always gave her, a glance that suggested she found Dot strange.

'Dorothy here is contemplating getting married,' Reverend Hawkins said with a stiff smile.

Estelle took in the information with no visible change of expression.

Hawkins turned to Dot. 'You don't mind me telling my wife, do you, my dear? We share everything. It's very important to us.'

'I'll leave you to help yourselves,' Estelle said wearily. She went out again without another word.

Hawkins became animated as he poured the tea, as if he were compensating for the brief, negative presence of his wife. 'I suspect that before you came here tonight, you may have been surer than you thought, Dorothy – about getting married, I mean. What you needed, I believe, was my approval.' He picked up a teaspoon. 'Sugar?'

'Three please.'

He spooned in the sugar with the precision of a chemist. 'Yes, my approval. But as I've indicated, I can't wholeheartedly grant that. You see, I would need to know

47

more – more about this young man, as well as more about your true feelings for him.'

Dot took the cup and saucer from Hawkins and set it on the table beside her chair. 'I think I've told you all I know about my feelings for Charlie,' she said. 'He makes me happy. I feel safe with him.'

'But is that enough?'

Dot hesitated, then said, 'It is for me, I think.' What more was there to want?

Hawkins tasted his tea, wrinkled his nose and put down the cup. 'Can Charlie offer you security? What does he do for a living?'

'Oh, he does a bit of this an' that. Clever with his hands, he is. He's after another job, just at the minute . . .'

'So he's out of work?'

'Only for the time bein'.'

Hawkins shook his head. 'Hardly a time to get married, is it?'

She had said that to Charlie. But he had come back with the argument that if they waited for the time to be right, it never would be, because nothing was ever perfect. 'At least,' he'd said, 'we'd have each other. We'd be takin' on the world as a couple.' Dot wasn't too sure what he meant by taking on the world, but she had been moved by Charlie's intensity. He seemed determined that they would have a good, happy, solid life together. She glanced at Hawkins now, unable to offer the kind of answer he'd find acceptable. 'I just feel we'd be right together, whatever the little hardships . . .'

'You're letting your heart rule your head,' Hawkins said sternly. 'Very unwise. But . . .' He sighed. 'You're not the first young woman to come to me in this condition. I suspect my warnings will mostly fall on stony ground. Just promise you'll do this for me, Dorothy.' He came and stood squarely in front of her. 'Think hard. Imagine yourself in a few years time. Try to look into the future at least far enough to see if it's a life you truly want. Try to imagine your feelings for this man being put to the test. Find out if you have the *strength* for marriage.'

It sounded like a tall order, but Dot nodded. 'I'll do that, Reverend.' He had been right, she realized, when he'd said she only came to get his approval. She was ready now to defend the idea of marrying Charlie. Strenuously. Nobody would talk her out of it.

As she was leaving Hawkins reminded her again that she should take her time and rush into nothing. 'Marry in haste, and repent at leisure,' he said, making his wise scowl as he closed the door behind her. He turned and saw Estelle coming from the kitchen. 'I've done what I can,' he sighed. 'Dorothy Colwell's a difficult girl to advise, though. She hasn't the strongest of wills.'

'No will at all, as far as I can see.' Estelle shuffled past her husband and fetched the tray from the sitting room. 'A leaf in the wind, that one,' she said. 'She'll never be anything else.'

5

After chapel on Sunday the 10th of August, two weeks and a day after Charlie's proposal, Dot went round to see her mother. It was time, she'd decided, to tell Martha what was happening. She explained about Charlie, whom she had never mentioned before. She said how they'd been seeing each other regularly for a pretty long time, and after some hesitation she told Martha that he had asked her to marry him. She didn't mention that Charlie had been covered in blood and suffering from three cracked ribs at the time.

'He wants you to *marry* him?' Martha sat hunched at the table, both hands wrapped round a coffee mug. The news, up to that point, had produced one of her more irritating bouts of incredulous head-shaking and eye-rolling. 'Are you sure you didn't pick him up wrong?'

'No Mum, I didn't get him wrong.' Dot was standing by the sideboard, still wearing her coat and hat and clutching her handbag, as if she might have to run at any second.

'What does he want you to do that for?'

'Because he wants me to be his wife, I suppose.'

'He must have a slate loose.' Martha put down her mug and sat back, folding her arms. 'What did you tell him?'

'I said I'd have to think about it. And I did. I went and asked Reverend Hawkins' advice, as well.'

Martha sniffed. 'So what's to happen?'

'I made up my mind I'd accept Charlie's proposal.'

'You what?'

'I told him yes I'd marry him.' Dot was colouring. She

tried to stare back at Martha, who was gaping at her with overdone dismay. 'What's wrong with that?'

'It's laughable. I mean you – married? It doesn't bear thinkin' about. You're not fit to run your own life, let alone see to a man an' look after a home an' do the million other things a wife has to do.' Martha waved a dismissive hand at Dot. 'Look at you. A bundle of nerves held together with skin. Head full of God an' sod-all else. What use'll you be to a man? What kind of bloke can he be, this Charlie, to want *you* for his ever-lovin'?'

'He's a nice, decent chap – '

'With a hump an' one eye, I shouldn't wonder.'

'Mum!' Dot snapped, trying to sound firm. 'I didn't come round here to collect another load of abuse.'

'Then what did you come for? A pat on the head? Eh? Did you want me to tell you how happy I am for you? Or did you just come to show off again?' Martha pushed back her chair and stood up. 'All you've done, my girl, is give me a worse headache than I had when you got here.'

'I'm sorry if that's the way you feel – '

'Well it is. Still . . .' Martha strode across to the kitchen area and perched on a stool with scabbed chrome legs. She folded her arms again. The added distance between herself and Dot seemed necessary, perhaps because it was easier to shout abuse across a decent-sized gap. 'While you're here, you might as well give me all the details, so I'll have no more shocks.'

'There's not a lot else to tell you.' Dot was making an effort to calm herself. Before she came out she had taken one of the Oblivon capsules the doctor had given her for her nerves. But she suspected it had worn off during Reverend Hawkins' sermon. She should have brought the bottle out with her and had another one before coming here. 'We're gettin' married in a couple of months' time. In the Methodist chapel, of course. There's a lot to sort out – a place to live, gettin' some sticks of furniture together an' so on.' Dot took a deep breath and let it out slowly, as if it might blow away the barrier of tension between herself and her mother. 'What I came here for, really, was to tell you that Charlie an' me hope you'll come to the weddin'.'

Martha's jaw dropped. 'Are you soft, or what? How can I go to a weddin'?'

Dot didn't see how she couldn't. She blinked at her mother, sure there was more to come.

'Where would I get the money for clothes?' Martha's voice was rising. 'Have you any idea when I last had anythin' new to wear? How can I turn up at the chapel wearin' the kind of rags the dustman wouldn't take away?'

'You've got that nice brown outfit – '

'I've had that the best part of ten years!' Martha screeched. 'An' I'd want somethin' a bloody sight cheerier than brown for a weddin' – even your weddin'!'

'Well . . .' Dot felt helpless. She should have known better than get herself into this. But she'd had to. How could she make plans to get married and not tell her own mother?

'An' what about the kids?' Martha demanded. 'Are they to turn up like ragamuffins? How would it look, eh? On your weddin' day, your whole family turnin' out like a bunch of tinkers.'

Dot said nothing. She couldn't think of anything.

'I can just see it,' Martha said, with the trace of a whine now. 'Me an' the kids bein' pointed at an' whispered about. The poor relations. I daresay you'll have yourself all decked out on the big day, though. No expense spared, I'll bet. I suppose that's what you've got in mind, invitin' us just so you can show us up. Let everybody see how much better you are than the rest of your family.'

'That's not true.' Dot was starting to shake.

'I know it's not true! You're not a patch on the other kids, rough an' ready as they are!'

'I meant – '

'An' I suppose there'll be a show of presents an' all. Ours'll look fabulous among the rest, eh? That's another way of humiliatin' me, of course. All the fancy bibs an' bobs laid out for inspection, an' right in the middle of it a soddin' butter dish out of Woolies – which is about as much as you can expect, with what I've got to live on.' Martha leaned forward, clutching the edge of the sink. 'That's you all over, intit? When you're not deliberately makin' me feel bad you're thinkin' about nobody but yourself. Surely you could've seen the spot you were puttin' me in, gettin' married?'

Dot sagged. She was too close to tears to argue. 'I'm sorry. Forget I ever mentioned the weddin'. I just thought it would've been nice to have you there. We both did . . .'

Martha shot off the stool and came darting across the room. She confronted Dot across the width of the table. 'What's this you're sayin' now?'

Dot stared at her, bewildered.

'You're sayin' I can't go to the weddin', is that it?'

Dot shook her head. 'No, I . . . *you* said . . .'

'I can't go to my own daughter's weddin'. That's marvellous. Priceless. The final slap in the teeth, that's what it is.'

'But you said you hadn't the clothes, or the money for them . . .'

Martha looked as if she had been slapped. 'I imagined you were goin' to do somethin' to help out in that direction, since it was you that invited us.'

Dot's head ached with confusion. 'Mum – I need all the money I've got. Charlie's not got a job an' both our savin's will hardly be enough to get us what we need.'

Martha began to nod. She went on nodding until Dot thought it would drive her mad. 'So,' Martha finally growled, 'it's a toerag you're marryin'. A layabout. I might've known nobody else would have anythin' to do with you.'

Tears surged forward, blinding Dot as she spun and half-ran into the passage, one hand clamped over her mouth. She tripped on a hole in the rug and nearly fell, then righted herself and pulled open the door. Her mother was yelling something after her, something she couldn't hear and didn't want to. She slammed the door and ran along the passage, not stopping until she was at the corner of the street.

She realized people were looking at her as she stood there whimpering and dabbing her eyes with her handkerchief. When would all this end? she wondered miserably. Was this all there was – unhappiness, endless hardship and strife? Charlie had told her there would be great times, happy times, when they had settled into their life together. She could believe it when he was with her, when there was his presence to back up his assurances. But at times like now, alone, being buffeted, Dot could hardly believe her life would ever improve. She sometimes believed God had singled her out for special suffering. She wished she understood His reasons better. She wished, devoutly, that he would grant her spirit a little more peace.

In the weeks leading up to the wedding Charlie Cotton worked hard at turning himself into a responsible citizen. He found a job, labouring to a spray-painter in a coach-building works. The pay was modest – seven pounds for a fifty-four hour week – and the work was unpleasant, because he was breathing acetate fumes all day and his skin got stained by the paint, and because the man he worked under was loud and aggressive and he obviously didn't like Charlie. But it was a job, and he drew a measure of pride from the discipline and the weekly wage packet.

He also found a place for Dot and himself to live. It was a single room, but a large one, at the top of a terraced house near his work. For three pounds-ten a week they would have to share a bathroom with four other couples, though the place was furnished with a bed, a cooker, sink and drainer, three kitchen chairs, two armchairs and a table. There was even a gas fire with a meter alongside. Charlie knew Dot's reaction to the place was less than ecstatic, but as he pointed out to her, it was a start, their first little nest, the place where they could make their plans for a bigger and better future.

On the Friday night before the wedding Charlie had his stag party. Dot didn't want him to do it. She had nothing against the celebration itself, but she didn't want Charlie to drink. Alcohol, as the minister had often said, was a demon, a genuine devil that got into men's blood and turned their brains towards madness and evil. She had shown Charlie leaflets about it and he had agreed with most of what he read. Or he said he did. But a stag night was different, he told Dot. It was a chap's farewell to the bachelor state, a cheerful renunciation of the free and easy life. It was fitting, too, that he could make his last night as a bachelor his last night as a drinker, too. In future there would be no drinking, Charlie promised; there would be no more carousing with the lads, either. The stag night would mark the end of an era.

The party kicked off in the Oak Leaf where Charlie, at sixteen, had drunk his first pint. After an hour they moved on to the Queen Victoria on the corner of Bridge Street and Albert Square, where Charlie had had his first legal pint at the age of eighteen.

'I reckon,' Ricky Johnson said, 'we should make this a real stag night.' He was propped on the end of the bar, brandishing a pound note as the barmaid pulled the drinks. 'The kind a bloke remembers through all the dark, dismal years of marriage.'

Charlie ignored him. He was still cool towards Ricky, after the screw-up on Oxford Street. It wasn't that they didn't talk any more – otherwise Ricky wouldn't have been invited along that evening. The fact was, Ricky's ever-thin credibility had fallen through. Word of his run-in with the Mob had travelled, and it had been noted that he hadn't dropped only himself in it. He'd involved a couple of mates as well. That kind of thing was never forgiven in Walford's semi-criminal community. The punishment was loss of status. Ricky was tolerated, but now he was the berk of the bunch, a has-been.

The other three members of the troupe at the bar – Tubby Perkins, Joe Hinds and Des Shilton – paid as little attention to Ricky's remark as Charlie did.

'Listen, Charlie,' Tubby said; 'does this mean we won't be havin' our Saturday nights out any more?'

Joe, small and thin and already turning bald, was nodding at Tubby. 'That's about the size of it, I reckon. This is the big curtain-up on marriage and the curtain-down on the good old days.'

'We've had some right old times together,' Des said. 'Haven't we?'

All three had been pals of Charlie's since school days. Tubby and Joe had stuck close all along; nowadays they were partners in a roof-repair business. Des, the youngest of the group, worked in a hotel kitchen.

'There'll be changes, certainly,' Charlie said.

'There's been a few already,' Tubby murmured. 'That's the big catch with women. They have to change a bloke. Can't let him stay as he is.'

'You won't have any troubles in that direction,' Des said. The others laughed. Tubby never denied that his size worked against him where women were concerned.

'Right, you bunch.' Ricky turned from the bar and

waved his hand along the row of full pint glasses. 'Start gettin' that lot down you.'

For the fourth time that night Charlie was toasted loudly, then mouthfuls of ale were sunk and the group set about finding a place to sit. As they squeezed themselves into the corner seats Ricky began slapping his hand on the table, like a chairman calling for order.

'It's home-truth time,' he said, grinning at the others. 'Cards on the table, eh?'

Tubby and Joe were talking about something else, paying no attention to Ricky. Des and Charlie were frowning at him. 'What're you on about?' Charlie asked.

Ricky gave him a music-hall wink. 'We're your mates, so we've a right to know.'

'Know what?'

'Aw come on,' Ricky groaned. 'It's the burnin' question at any stag do.' He leaned across the table. 'Have you or haven't you?'

'Eh?'

'Done it,' Ricky hissed. 'Have you had it away with her?'

'Of course I haven't.'

'Come off it . . .'

'She ain't that kind of girl,' Charlie insisted.

'They're all that kind of girl.'

'Then this one's different from all the rest.'

'Oi, oi,' Tubby cut in, 'what's all this?' He was forever suspicious of Ricky, whom he regarded as a troublemaker and definitely a couple of cuts beneath the rest of them. 'What are you barneyin' about?'

'This one reckons his bride-to-be's not the kind that slips a fella a bit in advance,' Ricky said.

'So?'

'So I reckon he's bullshittin'.'

There was an ugly, taunting note in Ricky's remark. In one sentence he had taken the lighthearted tone out of the gathering. Tubby reached across and closed his fingers round Ricky's elbow. To the others it looked like a simple cautioning gesture. What Ricky felt was a fearfully tight clamp.

'Just drop it, eh?' Tubby said.

'Christ, all I said was – '

'Drop it.' Tubby withdrew his hand, but he kept on staring at Ricky, his eyes issuing a steady warning.

Ricky stared back for a couple of seconds, then he stood up. 'Sod this.' He pushed out past little Des. 'I'm not stickin' around at no old women's tea party. I'll find myself a bit of fun some place else.' He paused, looking at Charlie. 'Some husband you're goin' to make. Can't even take a bloody joke.'

'Sit down, Ricky,' Charlie said. 'There's no need for us to fall out . . .'

'Let him go,' Tubby grunted.

Ricky went, pushing his way through the crowd at the bar. Tubby sighed and sat back. 'That's better,' he said. 'I can never relax when that bugger's about.'

For the next ten minutes, as the talk wandered aimlessly and they all began to laugh again, Charlie felt himself increasingly isolated, outwardly joining-in but somehow separate from the others. It was like being in a glass cocoon. He supposed the feeling had begun right at the start, when they had met at the other pub. For weeks he had been getting ready for this time, the bowing-out. He realized now that compared to the reality of this evening, the lead-up had been more of a game than anything.

It's happening, he thought. He was right on the threshold of the new life, the solid, responsible existence he'd yearned for. That terrible night, turning up at Dot's place with his body feeling like it had been through a harvester, the desire to abandon the old life had been so powerful he had felt it as a pain quite distinct from all the others. He had pleaded with Dot to marry him, to make it possible for him to reform and get out of the deepening, dead-loss rut he was in. Now it was about to happen, he was on the verge of stepping across the threshold into a positive, respectable, hard-working life with the woman he loved. But he wondered, increasingly as the time passed, if he really wanted it after all.

'Are you all right, Chas?' Joe asked.

Charlie blinked. He had been drifting off, going reflective. 'Yeah, I'm fine.'

'Sup up then, an' I'll get us another round in.'

The old life wasn't so bad, Charlie thought. He only had to look at the lads around the table to know that. They were happy enough. They didn't have many responsibilities. They weren't shackled to promises.

'Did you know Larry Slocum'd got married?' Des asked the assembled company. Larry had been another one of the old school crowd, but he had moved away from Walford in the mid-fifties. 'I met him an' his missus at the dog track a couple of weeks back. He'd got a couple of animals runnin'.'

'What's his wife like?' Tubby asked.

Des shook his head sadly. 'He's got one more dog about the house now, by the look of her. I didn't know anybody could be that ugly with only one head.'

Charlie felt himself flinch. Tubby had touched the same nerve Ricky had. Would they talk the same way behind his back? By now Charlie knew the others didn't see Dot in quite the same light as he did. They were diplomatic, of course. They never said anything uncomplimentary about her in front of him – not before tonight, anyway, and Ricky had only spoken the way he did because he was half-pissed and over-keen to play the big man again.

Charlie sighed quietly. He could tell the lads thought Dot was a bit odd. It would have been impossible to make them see differently, to explain the qualities he detected in her. How could he describe the way that the

59

meeting of their eyes, always so brief, made him tingly and syrupy inside? How could he convey the grace he sensed under even her most awkward movements? Hardest of all would be to describe the effect she had on him sexually. It was a special, inexplicable chemistry.

But there was a snag, and it was at the root of Charlie's uneasiness tonight. As the date of the wedding drew nearer he'd felt he should broach the subject of sex. He'd asked Dot, in the least blunt way he could, if she knew much about the physical side of married life. She told him she didn't want to talk about it. More than that, she'd managed to convince him, by her flustered, embarrassed response, that she knew nothing at all about sex and that she wasn't keen to learn. That was easy enough to believe – the most intimate contact between them, to date, had been one long kiss that Charlie had more or less forced on her. She didn't mind holding hands, or walking arm-in-arm. To anything closer or warmer she was stiff and unresponsive.

That worried Charlie. It had made him look beyond his adoration and wonder if he was marrying a frigid woman. Love could overcome a lot, he had told Dot that and he knew she believed him, but he wondered . . .

Joe had brought across more drinks. The landlord, Alf Barrett, came behind him, carrying two of the glasses. He put them down and beamed at Charlie. 'So, you're tyin' the knot, I hear.'

'That's right,' Charlie said, trying to look cheerful. 'Happens to us all in the end, I suppose.'

'Of course it does. An' all jokin' aside, it's the best thing that can happen to a man, if he works at it. It was the makin' of me, I don't mind tellin' you. I've no regrets. None.'

Charlie hung on to his grin and nodded. He was having his regrets right now, even before he was married. He looked at the lads, free and enjoying themselves, then pictured himself weighed down with responsibilities, spending his nights in a cold bed. It had all seemed so worthwhile at the beginning. He had ached for it.

As he shook Alf Barrett's hand and accepted his good wishes, Charlie thought hard, trying to muster the warm image of Dot that usually banished his uncertainty. But at that moment he couldn't see her face. All that came to him was her voice, asking him to promise he wouldn't drink too much.

6

The first fourteen months of marriage made changes in Dot, though few of them showed. Acquaintances still saw her as the spiky, nervous, frequently shrill person she had been in her single days. Marriage to Charlie Cotton didn't seem to have given her any change of manner or outlook. She still attended chapel, still worked in the sweet factory and showed no signs of abandoning her early-fifties pattern of dress and hairstyle. But inside, in the anxiety-ridden mind and spirit of the woman who couldn't get used to being called Dot Cotton, the changes were profound. She had learned new kinds of fear. She was prey to bouts of self-disgust, and she lived with constant foreboding.

The changes began on her wedding day. Fumbling her way through the responses at the altar had been traumatic enough, especially since she got the words wrong so many times that the minister had hissed at her under his breath, telling her to pull herself together. But afterwards, at the reception in Charlie's Aunt Maude's house, she saw a side of Charlie's nature that stunned her. The shock of the event still reverberated more than a year later, even though she had learned worse things about her husband since then.

Fifteen or sixteen people were at the reception, mostly relatives and friends of Charlie. After a while Dot found herself standing in a corner of the living room, nibbling a sandwich as she talked to Aunt Maude's daughter, Nell, a heavily made-up young woman with mobile eyes and fluttery hands. Nell was doing most of the talking.

'I always knew there was somethin' odd about Eric.

Even when I thought there was nobody like him in the world, I kept wonderin' what it was – this oddness, this somethin' unusual, you know?'

She had been talking about her ex-boyfriend for nearly five minutes, detailing the history of their relationship, working her way slowly to the reason for their split-up. Dot was only half paying attention. She kept watching her mother, who had turned up at the wedding alone and grim-faced, wearing the pink coat and dress Dot had paid seven pounds towards. Martha was looking less stern now, talking to Aunt Maude and another woman and gulping back sweet sherry. Dot hoped her mother wouldn't make any kind of scene, or say anything to upset her on her big day.

'When I found out what it was with him,' Nell went on, 'I nearly died. I mean I was close to Eric, really *close,* so you can imagine what it done to me.'

Dot frowned. 'What what done to you?'

'Findin' out about Eric, of course.'

Dot felt she'd missed something. 'What was it you found out?'

Nell looked about her. 'Well . . .' She stepped closer. 'How it happened, I went round to his place one night, an hour early on account of I'd got off work at four because we'd had a power cut, an' I let meself in – I'd a key, you see, because as I said we were real *close*, and as soon as the door opens I hear all this loud music. Really blarin' it was. Paul Anka, that Diana thing, Eric was dead keen on it. Played it all the time.' She glanced across the room to where one of her cousins, a fat boy with big gaps in his teeth was opening a fresh bottle of sherry. 'Excuse me a minute, love,' Nell said. 'I'll just snatch another drink while there's one goin'. Sure you'll not have one?'

'No thanks.'

'Not even on your weddin' day? Just one little sherry?'

'Sherry makes me bilious.'

'Okeydoke. I'll be back in a second.'

Dot was getting a headache. Her feet hurt in her new shoes, too. She was dying to sit down with a nice cup of tea; she always got a headache and felt a bit listless if she went too long without tea. Nell's chatter wasn't helping her head any, and the strain of keeping an eye on Martha was getting to be too much. Dot wished Charlie was with her, giving some moral support. But he had gone somewhere with his Uncle Bill; they had something to collect, Charlie had said, and he promised they wouldn't be long, but nearly an hour had passed and there was still no sign of them.

Nell came back. 'Where was I?'

'There was all this music,' Dot said. 'Blarin'.'

'Oh, yeah. So I goes into the lounge, not expectin' to find anythin' out of the ordinary. Just Eric sittin' on his tod with a beer, lappin' up the music. Well, he was sittin' on the couch sippin' a beer, all right. But there was another fella in there. Sittin' beside Eric. He was drinkin' beer an' all an' waggin' his nut to the music. But guess what else?'

Dot tried to guess. She gave up after a couple of seconds. 'I've no idea.'

'They was holdin' hands.'

'Really?' This was foggy territory for Dot. She had overheard the occasional whispered remark about nancies, but nothing she'd heard made any sense to her. It did seem very odd, though, that men should hold hands.

'It was the biggest blow of my life, Dot. I marched straight out of there an' I haven't seen him since.'

Dot wondered what she would do if she walked into a room and found Charlie holding a man's hand. Just look away, probably. Pretend she hadn't noticed.

Nell was about to enlarge on her terrible discovery when there was a bang out in the hallway. Everybody

64

went quiet. Aunt Maude stared round the room, questioning everybody with her eyes. Dot glanced away guiltily, as if it was her fault. A moment later the sitting room door was pushed open. Uncle Bill appeared, clearly the worse for drink. He smiled, turning a half circle to take in everybody.

'Where have you been?' Aunt Maude demanded.

'Gettin' the ale.'

'Decided to carry it in your belly, did you?'

A few people tittered. Uncle Bill's smile widened. 'We had a few with the guv'nor.'

'You promised to be right back.' Aunt Maude went to the door and looked into the hall. 'My God,' she said, stepping back. 'What happened to you?'

Charlie came into the room. He was smiling too. His hair was tousled, his tie was half undone and the sleeve of his jacket was ripped. 'Fell over gettin' the crate out of the taxi,' he said.

'Fell over gettin' *in* the bloody taxi too, if you'll remember.' Uncle Bill chuckled. 'He's had more whiskies bought him today than he's sunk all year.'

Dot dropped her sandwich and clapped a hand over her mouth as Charlie swayed across the room towards her mother. Martha was glaring at him with open and none-too-sober disdain.

'Hello again, Mrs Colwell.' Charlie made a comic little bow and staggered forward a step. 'Nice to see you're enjoyin' yourself.'

Aunt Maude was hustling Uncle Bill through to the kitchen to give him a talking-to. The other guests were resuming conversations and going neutral, aware that an embarrassing confrontation was brewing over by the window. Dot stood frozen, her hand still sealing her mouth, eyes wide as her mother carefully put down her sherry glass and squared up to Charlie.

'You're a drunken sot,' Martha hissed. 'You ought to be ashamed of yourself.'

Charlie pulled himself to his full height and frowned at her. 'I can hold my drink,' he said. 'An' besides, I'm celebratin', ain't I? I got married today.' He stuck his chin out. 'Or hadn't you noticed?' The chin came out further still. 'Or did you forget?'

Dot let out a muffled squeak.

'I'm not likely to forget this day,' Martha snapped. 'How could I forget my daughter marryin' a whisky-swillin' lump that's no good to himself or anybody else? Some son-in-law. You're a piggin' disgrace.'

'Flatterer.' Charlie swayed. 'But I have to say you did get the best of the bargain, darlin'. I mean look at what I got for a mother-in-law.'

'You mind your bloody gob!'

Charlie shook his head sorrowfully. 'You know what you look like with that clobber an' the hairdo? You're like a pink-handled loo brush.'

'I'm warnin' you!' Martha's face was purple. 'One more bloody word of slander – '

'Aw, blow it through your arse.' Charlie turned and walked out of the room, barely missing the door jamb.

'You'll need your prayers from now on, my girl!' Martha glared at Dot as she did up her coat and snatched her handbag off a chair. 'You'll have nothin' but grief with that pig!' She turned, waggled her head at the rest of the company and stamped out.

Nell was still standing beside Dot, staring at her. 'Are you all right? You don't want to go lettin' people put you in a state like that.' Dot was shaking, supporting herself against the wall with one hand. She was trying to speak but couldn't. 'Come on . . .' Nell put an arm round her shoulder. 'Let me take you to the bedroom. You can sit in there until you settle a bit.'

Dot wriggled away from her. 'I want Charlie,' she wailed. 'Where is he?' She ran out into the hall. 'Charlie!'

Nell shrugged at the others. 'She suffers with her nerves.'

Aunt Maude and Uncle Bill were slanging each other in the kitchen. Dot stood blinking at them for a second then turned back along the hall.

'Charlie! Where are you?'

She thrust open a bedroom door and saw him at once. He was standing at the window, looking out.

'Oh, Charlie . . .' Dot stumbled across to him, half-crying, clutching the curtain as she craned her neck to see his face. 'What did you have to do that for? You've gone an' spoiled everythin'.'

He didn't look at her. 'There wasn't a lot to spoil, was there,' he grunted. 'Piss-poor weddin'. Worst bloody weddin' I've ever been to.'

'Don't talk like that!'

Charlie's head jerked round. 'Don't talk like that!' he said, mimicking Dot's whine. 'How else do you expect me to talk? I go out an' have a few drinks on my weddin' day, just like any bloke would, I get a little bit merry, then I come back an' get treated like shit by the bride's lovely old mum. Just for havin' the brass neck to enjoy myself.'

'Charlie, this isn't like you – '

'She's a right cow, that mother of yours. Never liked the look of her. Not from the first minute I laid eyes on her. Know somethin'? I was about an inch from layin' one on her.'

Dot was fingering her mouth like a scared child. 'I've never seen you like this before.'

'You're seein' me like it now.'

'It's the drink. That's what it is. Drink. You know it's no good, I can't understand why you touch the stuff.'

'Dot. Listen.' Charlie took her by the shoulders. He

put his face close. His breath smelt powerfully of whisky as he drew back his lips, baring his teeth at her. 'If you're goin' to go on talkin' like this, you can bugger off along with your old lady.'

'Charlie!'

'I mean it!'

The shock of discovering Charlie's harsher side wasn't the last emotional injury Dot suffered that day. At ten minutes past eleven, in a seaside hotel room that had cost them ten pounds for the two days of their honeymoon, they stood facing each other across the bed. Charlie was in maroon pyjamas with yellow piping. Dot had on a quilted nylon dressing gown over a white winceyette nightdress with blue flowers on it. She had undressed in the bathroom along the hall.

'Well then,' Charlie said. He had sobered considerably, partly from the lecture his aunt had given him, partly from the stimulant effect of four cups of black Nescafé and the passage of time. 'We've made it. Married. How does it feel?'

Dot made a little shrug, her hands clutching the lapels of her dressing gown, drawing them close to her neck. 'It's all right.' She twitched a smile at Charlie then looked away. Her gaze landed on the bed and jumped smartly to the dressing table. She had taken three Oblivon, all at once, but she was still terrified.

'Will I get in first, or will you?' Charlie grinned. 'Or will we get in together?'

Dot shrugged again.

Charlie looked at her for a moment, then he came round the bed and put his arms around her. 'Nervous, are you?'

'A bit, yes.'

Charlie nuzzled her hair. He put his mouth close to her ear and nipped at the lobe. His right hand came away from her shoulder and slid down along her side. The fingers spidered slowly back and spread, enclosing one clenched buttock.

'Relax, love. Relax.'

He began kneading at her, his hand moving round her thigh, inching in under the dressing gown.

'Shall we get in bed?' Dot said in a strangled voice.

'Well, if you're invitin' me . . .' Charlie leered at her and moved away. He pulled back the covers. 'After you.'

With shaky fingers Dot undid her dressing gown and slipped it off. She couldn't meet Charlie's eyes as she climbed into the bed, clutching the hem of her nightie as it threatened to slide up. She grabbed the covers and pulled them over her.

'There you are, then. Snug as a bug.' Charlie went to the other side of the bed and started to get in.

'You've forgotten the light.'

Charlie paused with one knee on the bed. 'I thought we might leave it on for a bit.'

Dot's face went stiff. 'I think I'd sooner have it off.'

'Just what I was thinkin'.' Charlie leered again. 'Come on, Dot. We're married. It's all right. Anythin' we do is all right, now. It's legal.'

Dot's eyes were pleading. 'Charlie, please . . .'

He groaned. 'All right. We'll do it your way. For now.'

A week before, forcing herself to contemplate this moment, Dot had been unable to imagine what would happen. She knew, in the vaguest way, that men and women united bodily when they were married. She had even heard her mother and her stepfather doing it. It sounded painful, from all the moaning her mother did, but the act was sanctioned by God so it had to be all right, really. It was her duty as a wife to submit to it. All she could do was hope she would do it right. And she hoped it wouldn't hurt her too much.

For a while, after the light went out, she began to believe she would like it. In the darkness Charlie held her and caressed her gently; he whispered soft sounds in her ear and gave her the comforting, enclosing warmth of his body. Dot began to feel a great softening in herself. She had never felt so soothed and safe in her life.

Then it all changed. Charlie's movements became rough, urgent. He began panting, clutching at her, grabbing her hands and making her do things she didn't want to do. Dot became frightened again.

'Move!' Charlie grunted at her ear. He was spreadeagling her, handling her like something inanimate without feelings. 'Move, for Christ's sake!'

Sudden pain made Dot cry out. Charlie paid no heed. He plunged at her, snarling, sounding more like an animal than a man. The pain tore through Dot as her body was submitted to more violence than she could ever have imagined.

When it was over Charlie lay panting on her, smothering her with his weight. Dot lay clamping her lips with her teeth, wondering how anything so fierce, so agonizing and coarse, could ever be desired by any woman. How could the Lord ordain such an act – and how could it be called worshipping her husband with her body?

After a long time, during which he did no more than pant and grunt, Charlie rolled away from Dot and curled on his side with his back to her. In the dark Dot remained motionless, slow tears wetting her face. The pain was terrible. The loneliness was almost as bad. Was this what wedded bliss amounted to? She cried herself to sleep.

Some time later she woke suddenly, believing she was being beaten. Her brain cleared and she realized he was doing it again, hurting her as he growled and grunted and thrust himself at her. He didn't even know she was awake. Perhaps he didn't care.

The year was nearly over. Their first wedding anniversary had been two months ago. The changes in Dot had accumulated to a point where stress had whipped her into full-scale hypochondria. She had regular migraines, panic attacks, bouts of claustrophobia and depressions. Sex was no less of a nightmare now than it had been at the beginning. She had no social life and no sense of security; Charlie managed to spend any spare money they ever had, and although he said he was trying to give up drinking he still regularly dropped in at the pub on his way home from work. Some nights he didn't get back until shutting time. He went out on Saturday nights, too. Whenever Dot tackled him on his promise to give up booze, he would say he really was trying, but the awful job he had, plus the pressure of trying to find a better job and a better place to live were strain enough, without him having to turn into a teetotaler overnight.

Dot feared for the future. She saw no signs of anything getting better for them. Other people, girls she worked with, seemed to move ahead in their marriages. Their husbands got promoted at work or found better-paid jobs; they got nice houses, proper homes, and they could buy nice things for them. Dot and Charlie were still in their draughty single room. Nothing in it had changed, except to get older. Saddest of all, though, was that Dot's dreams had dissolved into nothing. Her prince, her Charlie, didn't even seem to like her much any more. All the things they had talked about and planned, the strength Charlie had said they would find together and the happiness their marriage would give them – none of that had happened, or even begun to happen. Dot had been unhappy as a child and never very happy as a young unmarried woman. Now, she was sure, she had never been so thoroughly unhappy in her life.

On a cold Saturday night in November, waiting for Charlie to get home from the pub, she sat by the gas fire and listened to the news on the wireless. It had become a regular practice. She never took much of it in, but it

71

made a sound in the room, another human voice. She heard that the last British troops had left Jordan; Ghana and Guinea would form the nucleus of a union of West African states; throughout Europe, 160 electronic computers were already in use. Dot reached out suddenly and switched the wireless off. Tonight, the newsreader's voice was only an irritation. She got up and sat at the table, feeling the tingle of an approaching migraine. If she didn't exert herself too much, it might not come on.

She looked at the clock. It would be another hour and a half, at least, before Charlie got back. She wished he would come in now, while she had the strength in her, the nervous drive to tell him what she had been avoiding telling him. Sometimes it was like that; she could suddenly find it in herself to blurt something out, whatever the consequences.

She was too fidgety to sit. She got up and went to the window. There was nothing much to see beyond the darkened glass, but it was a different panorama, a change from chipped furniture and faded wallpaper.

What would he say, she wondered? She couldn't imagine him being glad – although it was wrong to judge ahead. Maybe the news would work a miracle in him. Perhaps it would turn him into the kind of man he'd said he would be when he was married.

Dot sighed. She would know soon how he'd take it. It had to be tonight, she didn't think it was doing her health any good, keeping it bottled up. She gazed down at the street lights, letting her eyes go off-focus and imagining he was there in the room with her.

'Charlie,' she said, 'I've got something to tell you. I'm going to have a baby.'

In the echoing old room it sounded odd and hollow, like no kind of news at all. She started to wonder again what Charlie would feel about it, then stopped herself. What was the point? She didn't even know how she felt about it herself.

7

Christmas Eve was a Wednesday. That meant it was going to be a long holiday, since most people in Walford had knocked off work at lunch time on Christmas Eve and wouldn't be expected back until after Boxing Day, which conveniently fell on a Friday.

'A five-day thrash,' Tubby Perkins said. 'Lovely. Then two days off the pop to sober up for New Year's Eve. It'll be a while before we get a deal like this again.'

'All right for them that can afford it,' Charlie said.

Tubby slapped his shoulder. 'I'll see you all right for a few bob, kid. Joe an' me's had a good year.'

They were in The Queen Victoria, having an impromptu pre-Christmas drink. They had met outside at the Beale's fruit and veg stall, where young Ronnie Beale and his mother had been doing a hectic trade in brussels sprouts and nuts, selling mostly to last-minute-panic housewives. Tubby had been buying a fruit gift-basket for his mother; Charlie had been considering the purchase of some apples, just to brighten up the centre of the table over the festive season.

'Look at this place,' Charlie said. The promise of financial aid over the holiday had brightened him instantly. 'This is the way I like it. Jumpin'. Jovial. You can't beat the Queen Vic when it's busy. Gives you a warm feelin'.'

'I'll bet it gives Alf Barrett a warm feelin', all right.' Tubby grinned. 'That till drawer's been bangin' like a shithouse door since we came in.'

Alf heard. Like all landlords he had selective hearing. Even when the place was jammed to the doors he could

73

single out and listen to any conversation he wanted – especially if he heard his name mentioned. He came across and nodded to Tubby.

'All right, Alf?'

'Fine thanks, Tubby.' Alf issued another nod in the direction of Charlie. 'You're right,' he said, looking at Tubby again. 'I've got this real warm glow, right down in my wallet. It's my compensation for havin' to be at the beck an' call of any turd with a shillin' to spend.' He winked. 'I'm tellin' Polly she can have that new hat.'

'Good on you,' Tubby said. He jerked his thumb at a little woman on a stool halfway along the bar. She was somewhere in her middle to late thirties, dressed in a bright yellow blouse, green skirt and purple cardigan. 'It don't look like you'll be makin' much more profit out of her.' The woman was swaying on the stool, looking happy in a glazed way, smiling at thin air and waving her glass to the tempo of some tune in her head. 'I think she's had a bit more than her quota.'

'That's Ethel Skinner. No trouble, as a rule. But when her old man ain't around she tends to drink with both hands. He'll be here to see her home in a bit. In her way, Ethel's a gem.'

'Yeah,' Tubby said, full of Christmas magnanimity. 'They're a smashin' bunch round here.'

'With the odd exception.' Alf pointed beyond Ethel to a middle-aged man with both elbows on the bar. He was scowling into his beer glass as if it had said something nasty to him. 'I'd sooner have Ethel an' her kind any day than that miserable, thievin', anti-social old git.'

Tubby nodded. 'Reg Cox. He's never been any different, far as I can remember.'

'He's lifted punters' change off the counter twice since he came in. Twice that I know of, that is. Both times when I tackled him about it he starts actin' drunk an' sayin' he thought it was his.'

'Takes all sorts,' Tubby said, determined to stay benevolent.

Alf landed a soft punch on Charlie's arm. 'So how's married life, son? Must be a year an' more by now.'

'Quite a while now, yeah. Everythin's fine, thanks.'

'I told you it would be.'

A customer banged a glass on the bar and Alf went off to serve him. Tubby looked at Charlie, one eye narrowed. 'You should put in for actin' school.'

'What do you mean?'

'The way you told him things was hunkydory. Very convincin'.'

They had been meeting as regularly since Charlie and Dot got married as they had in the old days. After the first few months Charlie had started talking about his unrest, his dissatisfaction and his disillusionment.

'I can kid other people,' Charlie said. 'It'd be some trick if I could con myself.'

'I told you what you should do, didn't I?'

Charlie made a face at Tubby. 'Easy for you to say. You're not married.'

'It means I've got a clearer view of things, because I'm not involved. Look, if you've got a bad leg, a sore gut, a wart growin' on the end of your plonker – what do you do? You get it sorted out, don't you? You get cured. Even if it means some kind of amputation, you're better off gettin' cured. What you want to do is amputate what's botherin' you. Now that's not talkin' out of turn, you know that. I'm a mate, concerned about you. You've aged since you got married, an' that's straight. You mope about, your mind's always some place else an' there's hardly a laugh comes out of you.'

'I know, I know . . .'

'Get yourself sorted out,' Tubby said. 'It'd be great to have you back as one of the old crowd. *Properly* back, that is. Enjoyin' yourself. Able to have a pound or two in your pocket that's not spoken for. Christ Charlie, women are only women. You've got your mates forever.'

'Yeah, sure, I hear you . . .'

'So do somethin' about it.'

There was a momentary diversion as Ethel Skinner fell off her stool. Two men picked her up and propped her against the bar. In the meantime Reg Cox had finished her drink.

Tubby turned back to Charlie. 'Never a dull moment, eh?' He put his big round head on one side, examining his mate. 'Are you goin' to take my advice, or what?'

Charlie shrugged and spread his hands. 'I don't know. The thing is, we're not enemies, me an' Dot. I can't put my hand on my heart an' say I hate her or anythin' like that. An' in her way she's a good wife to me. It's not easy to be cold-blooded about sortin' things out . . .'

He shrugged again. How could he explain the presence of a dead dream in the midst of a living reality? He didn't have what he'd wanted, but he had *something*. It was complex. Dot's presence in his life caused him pain, but it was as if she belonged there. He had great pity for her, at times. At other times he was bewildered; how could he have believed, so fervently, that life was going to be a golden gravy train when he married her? One thing he did know, though – he had misjudged things badly. What he had imagined was hidden in Dot, only waiting to be released, wasn't there at all. It had been like pulling back a tantalizing curtain to discover there was nothing behind it.

'Drink up,' Tubby said. 'Your beer's goin' flat.'

Charlie emptied his glass and put it on the bar. 'I want to get off the subject, Tubby, because it's Christmas an' we should all be gettin' legless an' happy. But let me tell you this. I've a lot of pity for Dot. I know she's a nerve case, a religious nut an' frigid as an ice lolly. But she's had a terrible life.'

76

'We've all had our hard times,' Tubby said, trying to attract Polly Barrett's attention.

'Yeah, I know, but listen – Dot's had it harder than most. She was three when the war broke out. Her old man had been away in the army only four months when he was posted missin', presumed dead. Not long after, Dot was evacuated to a farm in Wales with her mum. Now get this – they'd only been in Wales six weeks when her mum ran off back to London an' left Dot behind. The war was over before the authorities located the cow an' made her take Dot back. In the meantime, mummy had got herself married again an' had another couple of kids.'

'Not the best of backgrounds,' Tubby admitted.

'From the age of nine until she left home, Dot had to bring them kids up, practically. There was no love for her at home, no affection. She was nothin' but a skivvy. It's not surprisin' she took to religion an' her nerves went to buggery.'

Tubby had finally been served. He pushed Charlie's drink towards him. 'Now you've got it off your chest we can drop the subject, eh? You're right, we should be enjoyin' ourselves instead of talkin' about your miseries.'

'Cheers.' Charlie sipped his pint. He had been tempted to add a footnote to Dot's story and tell Tubby that she was pregnant and going through hell. But he decided not to. So far he had told nobody, and he would leave it that way for as long as he could – at least until he didn't feel so mixed up at the idea of becoming a father.

'Well hello there, Tubbles.'

Charlie looked up from his drink and saw a girl approaching Tubby, her lips puckered ready for a kiss. She was about twenty, a blonde with a ponytail and a spectacular resemblance to Diana Dors.

'Judy! You look great!'

Tubby opened his arms and enclosed her against his

bulk. They kissed elaborately, then the girl extricated herself. She looked at Charlie and smiled.

'Introduce me to your friend then, Tubby.'

For the first time in ages Charlie found himself wondering how he looked. He was glad he had gone home first and changed out of his work clothes. He touched the knot in his slim-jim tie as Tubby made the introductions.

'Pleased to meet you, Charlie.'

'Same here, Judy.' Charlie shook her hand, feeling a little thrill at its softness and warmth. He looked at Tubby. 'You've been keeping this young lady a secret from the rest of us.'

'Judy's my cousin,' Tubby said. 'Lives in Manchester. We only ever see her at the holidays.'

'Oh.' Charlie's hand went to his pocket automatically. 'What're you drinkin', Judy?'

'No, no,' she said, flapping his offer aside. 'My treat – and besides, I've a couple of girlfriends with me. They're sitting over by the door.' She produced a purse from her voluminous handbag. 'What're you two lads having?'

Tubby pointed to the full pints in front of them. 'We've just got these in.'

'Then have some more. It's Christmas.'

Charlie shook his head. 'It's not fair, a girl havin' to buy drinks.'

Judy stared at him. 'How quaint. An old-fashioned gent. God, I must meet you again, Charlie. It's dead refreshing.' She came round to stand beside Charlie and order the drinks. When Alf Barrett had taken her order she turned to Charlie and said, 'I can tell by the way you're leaning there – this is your favourite local, isn't it?'

'I suppose it is.'

'I'm never wrong,' Judy said, smiling and showing small, even white teeth. 'Something about the way a chap relaxes in his favourite spot. It always shows.'

'Watched a lot of men in a lot of bars, have you?'

Charlie realized he had said that without thinking. In the old days, the pre-Dot days, that kind of patter had always come to him naturally.

'A few.' Judy gave him one of those looks, the kind he hadn't seen in a while. It was a fleeting narrowing of the eyes, accompanied by a similarly brief straightening of the features. It was shorthand for something that would have taken about a minute to say. 'I don't talk to them all, mind you.'

'I'm sure you don't. You're much too nice for that.'

Judy nodded. 'Not too nice, though. I'm no spoil-sport.'

The drinks came. Judy paid for them, took the tray with her three glasses on it and excused herself.

'I won't introduce my friends. They're a bit tiresome.' She wrinkled her nose. 'You know – married. It's a duty get-together. Thought I might as well do it straight away and get it over and done with.'

'You'll be round to Mum's over the holiday, won't you?' Tubby said.

'Of course I will.' Judy turned to Charlie. 'Will you be visiting Tubby's mum, at all?'

'I could make a point of it.'

'Well, I might see you.' The look again, then she said, 'Must trot. Enjoy yourselves.'

When she had gone Tubby turned to Charlie and winked. 'Some girl, eh? I'm glad she left the district when she did. I've fancied her since I was eleven. I'd have wound up givin' her one, even if she *is* family.'

'It's all right with cousins,' Charlie told him.

'Not in our bloody family it isn't.' Tubby picked up his pint, then put it down again. 'Tell me straight – she was givin' you the eye, wasn't she?'

'Could've been.'

'Could've my arse. She was.' Tubby chewed his lip for

a second. 'I reckon you could have pulled her, if you'd wanted to.'

'Don't put notions in my head, Tubby.'

But the notion was already there. Charlie couldn't remember when he had last felt so good. And all it had taken was a little bit of back and forth chat with a good looking girl. And a clear come-on, of course. He thought about that as he gulped his beer. It was a dizzying thought.

'There's nothin' like a bit of recreation,' Tubby murmured. 'Especially when a bloke's feelin' a bit low.' He winked again.

True enough, Charlie thought, even though conscience told him he shouldn't have thoughts in that direction. Whatever the rights and wrongs, though, nothing in him could deny that it would be good to have a diversion, just now and again. Something that would take his mind off things.

8

Dr Mulvaney was a psychiatrist who, in his own estimation, was working hard enough and long enough to put
himself into a mental institution. In the winter months, his
clinic at the King George VI hospital in Armitage Road,
Walford, was even busier than Maternity Outpatients for
some reason. Dr Mulvaney's wife blamed it on television.
More and more people were watching it, and they
watched more in the winter, and since it was obvious to
anyone that television depressed people, the cause of the
overcrowding in the psychiatrist's waiting room was no
mystery.

Looking at the case notes in front of him, Dr Mulvaney
reflected that TV couldn't be blamed for Mrs Dorothy
Cotton's troubles. She didn't have a set, and besides that,
her nervous disorders dated back to a time long before
post-war television came along. As far as Mulvaney could
tell, there was no single cause of her condition. There
was no single set of causes, either. He yawned as he
scanned the notes, refreshing his memory.

*A question arises as to whether the patient has a personality
disorder. She displays a rigid, exaggerated set of behaviour
patterns when she is under stress, or when she imagines
she is. There are strong indications of social and private
maladjustment, even though she believes that her behaviour
is normal and right – a classic symptom of personality
disorder. She is also strongly hypochondriac, which tallies
with the classic picture.*

Dr Mulvaney scratched his chin. That diagnosis was all
very well, but two weeks after he had made the notes he

made others that contradicted – or at least complicated – the first set.

> *The patient appears to have a powerful obsessive-compulsive neurosis. Ideas and images, usually unconnected to what she may be doing, force themselves on her and won't be dislodged. After much probing, it has been possible to determine that the patient entertains sexual notions and fantasies which she believes are quite foreign to her. They cause her much distress. To complete the picture of obsessive-compulsive behaviour, she experiences strong urges to do things which are entirely against her nature and ethics.*

So Mrs Cotton was a classic neurotic, as well as possessing a possibly disordered personality. That wasn't all. In the three months she had been attending the clinic, she had shown occasional signs of a hysterical neurosis; one of its features was an ability to mimic, without trying, the symptoms of a number of illnesses. As if that weren't enough, Dr Mulvaney had also found signs of Briquet's Syndrome, which was similar to hysterical neurosis, but which had enough distinct features to establish it as a separate illness.

Coming up with a treatment was difficult. Every time the doctor decided on a course of action, something the patient did or said would make him think again. He couldn't use drug therapy because of her pregnancy, so the answer for the present had to be purely psychiatric. Mrs Cotton was not good at accepting that kind of treatment. She had been referred to the clinic by her GP, who felt her depressions and anxieties had increased since she'd become pregnant. It hadn't been easy to get her to attend; when she started the sessions she was almost completely uncommunicative. The process of breaking down her resistance had been a long and tedious one. She seemed to like talking, now that she knew Mulvaney better, but there was an underlying mistrust that he couldn't budge. He had the feeling she regarded him as some kind of witch doctor.

He looked at his watch and sighed. There simply wasn't time to mull things over. It was after two and he had four patients to see after Mrs Cotton. Two of them would be time-consuming. Mulvaney hit the button on his desk and sat back, putting on his placid, reassuring face.

Dot came round the door cautiously, as she always did. She nodded at the doctor and showed him her front teeth, which was as close to a smile as she could ever muster in his presence.

'Good afternoon, Mrs Cotton. Come and sit down.' The couch was out of the question with Dot. He had tried it once but had to get her up and into a chair when she developed a panic attack. 'How have you been since we last talked?'

'About the same, Doctor.' Dot perched on the straight-backed chair and drew her handbag protectively against the small mound of her stomach. 'I've been havin' the headaches again quite bad. An' I'm not sleepin' at all well. Apart from that, I've been pretty good, I suppose.'

Mulvaney glanced at his notes. 'At our last meeting, just before our time was up, you mentioned that you'd the feeling someone was following you, every time you went out shopping.'

'No, no . . .' Dot shook her head. 'Not every time, Doctor. Only when I'm wearin' my tweed coat, for some reason.'

'I see. And has it happened recently – since we last met?'

'Oh yes. Three times.'

'And always when you've had on the tweed coat?'

'That's right.'

'So what happens? I mean do you actually look to see if there's anyone there behind you?'

'No,' Dot said. 'I never look.'

'Why not?'

'Because something bad would happen. That's what I feel, anyway.'

'Perhaps if you stop wearing the coat, the feelings will go away.'

'Oh, I can't do that either. Because if I stopped wearing it, or gave it away or got rid of it at all, something bad would happen then, too.'

Mulvaney nodded, deciding he wouldn't pursue that one. It sounded like paranoia and he had enough to handle. 'We'll talk about that some other time, I think. Today, I wanted to talk to you about relaxing a bit more. I've a feeling that a lot of your trouble's to do with being tense. Proper relaxation would make you feel better, and it's particularly important now that you're pregnant. The baby itself could be affected by tension, you see. It's now believed that behaviour problems in some children are due to the mother's relaxation difficulties during the months of pregnancy.'

Dot was nodding. 'The baby *is* a bit tense, I must say.'

'Pardon?'

'I can feel it. He lies very stiff.'

'Oh.' Mulvaney made a mental shrug. He might as well use that little delusion to advantage. 'There you are, then. For his sake alone, I think you ought to relax more. There are one or two little tricks you can use that'll help you to manage it.'

For five minutes he spoke to Dot about fundamental relaxation techniques. He told her about picturing a big clock and trying to time her breathing to the movement of its sweeping second hand. He mentioned the technique of relaxing her body a joint at a time, and picturing something soothing as she did that. He tried to make his voice a comfort to her as he spoke, a purring presence that she might recollect as she lay there at home, trying

84

to unclench her mind and body. Dot took it all in silently, wagging her head steadily, until Dr Mulvaney mentioned that it helped to have someone stroke the shoulders and neck regularly, especially at the end of the day, just before turning in.

'Chance'd be a fine thing,' Dot said, then blushed, her eyes darting about the room.

'I'm sorry?'

'Nothing. I just . . . Nothing.'

'Now remember what we agreed at the start,' Mulvaney reminded her gently. 'Nothing is to be kept covered up. Even the tiniest difficulty at home could have some importance in helping me to treat you.' He waited for a moment. 'Is there some problem at home?'

Dot rapped her fingers rhythmically on her handbag. Her gaze still wouldn't settle.

'Something between you and your husband?'

'I suppose so, yes.'

'Tell me about it. Take your time.'

The relationship of Dorothy and Charles Cotton was something Mulvaney hadn't probed as deeply as he might. What he had gathered, so far, was that they lived pretty humdrum lives domestically. They had become very used to each other, perhaps even found one another quite dull. That was the picture that had emerged anyway, and if anything else were the case Mrs Cotton hadn't come forward with evidence. She had insisted, with crimson cheeks, that she had no sexual difficulties, not of the marital kind anyway. With the welter of psychiatric evidence Mulvaney already had to cope with from this one patient, he had been content – and perhaps mistaken, he now thought – to accept that the Cottons' sex life was as ordinary and unexceptional as most other married couples'.

'Charlie's kind of distant to me,' Dot said, staring at the edge of the desk. 'I mean, you said about gettin' me shoulders an' neck rubbed at bedtime – well I never see him at bedtime.'

'Never?'

'Not for months. He gets in late. I used to wait up, but I get such a sore back in the evenin's now, I have to go to bed on my own.'

'Is it his work that keeps him late?' Mulvaney asked, knowing it would be nothing of the sort. She had used the word 'distant'. He had heard it often, from wives who had been isolated by their husbands' indifference.

Dot was toying with the clasp of her bag. 'It's other people that keep him out late. Charlie's not a bad man, Doctor, but he can be weak. He lets his friends lead him into things he wouldn't choose to do himself.'

'And when he *is* home – how is he then?'

Dot shrugged. 'It's me, I think. I'm the trouble at home. Other people are the trouble outside.' She sighed. 'Poor Charlie.'

'What do you mean when you say you're the trouble?'

'Well, carryin' the baby an' all – it's not easy for Charlie to put up with me. I get tired easily an' I'm terribly jumpy at times, an' of course I'm not the most fetchin' sight, am I?'

'Has he said that – that you don't look nice?'

She sniffed. 'He's made the odd remark. But usually he's had drink in him when he's said anythin', so I suppose those times don't count. Drink does terrible things to men's minds.'

Mulvaney was impressed with her capacity to blame herself so easily. Impressed and puzzled. It didn't line up with her flashes of paranoia, or a lot of the other symptoms she displayed. As a case study she was a fascinating paradox. As a woman she was a sad, bewildered soul, burdened with perplexities and taking on new ones practically every day, as far as the doctor could see.

'Tell me something,' he said, 'and don't be shy, it's

very important. How long has it been since your husband and you made love?'

The colour rushed to Dot's cheeks. 'Charlie's not much of a one for cuddlin' an' things like that . . .'

'No, I didn't mean that. I meant when did you last have intercourse?'

Dot gulped softly. 'I don't see what that has to do with anythin'.'

'It has a lot to do with a lot of things,' Mulvaney assured her. 'How long has it been?'

She said nothing for several seconds. 'A while,' she murmured at last.

'How long?'

'Six months or so.'

'Since the time you knew you were pregnant?'

Dot nodded.

'Haven't you wanted to? Has that been the problem?'

'I've never wanted to.' It had slipped out and Dot clenched her teeth, as if she wanted to stop it before it escaped into the air.

'And your husband,' Mulvaney said calmly. 'Has *he* wanted to – since he learned you were pregnant, that is?'

'No.'

'Are you sure?'

'I'm sure.'

Mulvaney looked at the clock on the wall behind Dot. To begin exploring this would take more time than they had at their disposal today. 'It's something we should look at carefully,' he said softly, 'but not today.' He noticed Dot looked instantly relieved. 'For the moment, I think we should go on talking about relaxation. I'm convinced you need to learn to put yourself at ease, and to do it regularly.'

'If you say so, Doctor.'

When the session was over and Dot left, promising she would spend at least twenty minutes every day doing her relaxation exercises, Dr Mulvaney drew her case notes towards him and uncapped his pen. He had no idea what he was going to write. All he was creating in that folder, he believed, was a growing list of disorders. There were no proposals for treatment, no trace of an entry that hinted at improvement. Just more symptoms, more conflicting and confusing evidence.

Finally, after chewing the end of the pen for a couple of minutes, he wrote, *Marital difficulties. Could be serious, since the patient appears to be frigid. Husband alienated, on the strength of present evidence. Sexual problems could underly a number of the patient's symptoms. Pro tem, physical and mental relaxation are being encouraged. No serious analysis is advisable from now until after Mrs Cotton's child is born, since such a course could prove stressful.*

Mulvaney dated the entry and recapped his pen. He seriously doubted if Mrs Cotton would continue seeing him after she'd had the baby. She would be too busy, too tied-down. Too unwilling. It happened often. He closed the folder and looked at it. Dorothy Cotton, he glumly felt sure, would continue to struggle with her nervous and psychological disorders for the rest of her days, without much useful help from anyone. All the case history represented was a partial record of her sorry state. A full record, if there could ever be one, would be a thick document indeed. And it would have nothing like a happy ending.

9

One night Charlie Cotton found himself in possession of seventy-five pounds. It was more money than he'd ever had at any one time. For a while after he got it he sat in a pub toilet and just stared at the bundle, passing the notes from hand to hand, fingering them, riffling them, folding them to see the wad they made.

After years of thinking that somebody up there loathed him, he felt this was a thumbs-up sign from some Providence that looked after the likes of him. When he was a kid his grandfather had told him, often, that perseverance always pays off. He'd been a lot older before he properly knew what perseverance was, and it had taken years and years for his grandfather to be proved right. But here was the proof. Seventy-five smackers. The reward of maybe a month's solid perseverance.

He would start using that phrase from now on. 'Perseverance always pays off.' He would say it with a slow wink and pat his hip pocket. Perseverance was the tool he had been looking for. All along he'd known there was a way into the jam stakes, the easy life, if only he could find it. Perseverance was the answer, all right. He'd had a pretty good feeling that something was working for him. The rewards as he went along had been small but steady; that had been enough to keep him trying.

'Bingo!' he hissed, sitting in the dank little toilet, hefting the loot one more time, then tucking it into his pocket. The big question now was, what would he spend it on? It was an awful lot, more than he'd ever made plans for. He thought about it for a minute or two, then decided the first thing was to go out and have one hell of a good time. He went back to the public bar to wait for some of his mates to show up. There was no point in trying to have a ball on his own.

The pub was The Angel, a place just off Walford High Road where Charlie's new mate Stretch Campbell liked to hang out. Stretch was a Jamaican with a line in racy patter and a wardrobe of suits, flash shoes and skinny-brim hats to rival any up West. Stretch was a sharp operator, and while he didn't actually acknowledge Charlie as an equal, he did welcome him into his circle and make him feel like somebody with potential.

Doing the cars had been Stretch's idea. Two things were essential for success, he had told Charlie – three things if you counted a white face, because the law were always watching the blacks. You needed some keys, and you needed to learn how to locate the right one quickly and use it without panicking. Thus equipped you were off and running. The trick was to pick cars in good class areas, and only on streets away from the main thoroughfares. It was essential to keep on the move, and never to do more than one car on any one street.

Charlie had picked up a fair amount of stuff during his first month. Most of it was fenceable, too. Briefcases had the most amazing variety of stuff in them. Glove compartments, too. Up to that night, when he had hit a jackpot, Charlie had made maybe sixty pounds total. Fifteen of it had to be used to pay for the keys Stretch had got him, but the rest was pocket money. He had kept Stretch posted on what he had hauled as the days went by. Tonight, he didn't think he would mention the cash. Certainly not how much it was. He didn't want Stretch or any of the other lads getting jealous and wanting to muscle in.

'How's it goin', Charlie?'

He turned from the bar and saw Letitia, Stretch's current girlfriend. She was rather tall for a girl, with even, pleasing features and dark razor-cut hair. She wore pale, chalky make-up which contrasted sharply – weirdly, Charlie sometimes thought – with the heavy mascara on her eyes. Tonight she had on white trousers, white high-heeled boots and a low-necked blue angora sweater. That was surprise number one, because she usually wore old corduroy skirts and high-necked sweaters or blouses. Surprise number two was that she was talking to Charlie without prompting, because she usually ignored him.

'Things're fine,' Charlie said. 'Couldn't be better.'

'In that case, you won't mind buying a girl a drink.'

'Yeah, sure.' Charlie looked round cautiously. One of Stretch's most notable features, besides his style and his chat, was his jealousy. Letitia was sacred territory. Anybody – *anybody* – who chatted her up or stepped out of line with her in any way was liable for a heavy warning, and maybe even a thick lip, depending on how much Stretch had had to drink. There was no sign of Stretch, though. Surprise number three – Letitia out on her own, unattended. 'Gin and Italian, right?'

'Right first time.'

Charlie got the drink and put it on the bar in front of her. 'Good health, then.'

'Cheers.' Letitia swallowed some and put the glass down. 'Hear about Stretch, did you?'

'Mm? No, I just got here. Nothin's happened, I hope?'

'Nothin' desperate. Twisted his ankle. They think he might've broke it. He was playin' silly buggers, jumpin' an' jivin' on some crates in his lock-up. Fell off one, the silly prat.'

'Oh dear.' Charlie shook his head and tut-tutted. 'Poor old lad. Where is he, then?'

'Laid up at home. His mum's feedin' him aspirins an' rum. He's in a bit of pain, but he's all right.'

'Well give him my best, when you see him.'

'Yeah, I'll do that.' Letitia picked up her drink again and took a gulp.

This was a bit of a blow, Charlie thought. He'd been starting to look forward to a great night with the lads. He could still do that, but it wouldn't be the same without Stretch.

'I was really fancyin' a bit of a caper tonight,' he told Letitia. 'You know, lettin' me hair down. Few pints, a few laughs, then finish up down the Indian restaurant for a bellyful of curry.'

'Sounds great.' Letitia sighed pointedly. 'I was lookin' forward to tonight a bit myself, as it happens. Fridays are different, aren't they? I mean you can really kick off the weekend on a Friday night.' She looked at Charlie. 'Still, there's nothin' to stop you, is there?'

'I suppose not.'

He thought about what he might do. Normally, he would have gone down the other end of Walford and looked up Tubby, Joe and Les. But they were pretty cool to him nowadays, since he'd started to pal with Stretch. He could have called up Judy, if she'd been in town that weekend. He believed she was another reason Tubby cold-shouldered him lately. Charlie reckoned Tubby was jealous. Tough. It had been Tubby that put the idea in his head in the first place.

Letitia sighed again, demonstrating a shade more unrest this time. 'Al and Banksie an' the rest of them have gone over to Putney. There's some knees-up or other goin' on at the Star an' Garter.'

That was just great. It meant none of the lads would be showing tonight. Charlie thought they might at least have told him. Here he was with a pocket full of dough and no mates to spend it on. He didn't fancy going over to Putney to join them. Charlie didn't like that area. It was another London all together, as far as he was concerned.

'If you're goin' on some place after this,' Letitia said,

92

speaking quietly and scarcely moving her lips, so the nosey barman wouldn't notice she was saying anything, 'would you mind if I tagged along?'

Charlie stared at her.

'Of course if I'd be in the way – '

'No, no, nothin' like that, Letitia.' Charlie swallowed and lowered his own voice. 'It's just that Stretch, you know, he doesn't like anybody interferin' – not that I'm sayin' I'm the sort of bloke to get up to anythin', but it might be hard convincin' him, know what I mean?'

'How would he find out, if we went somewhere away from the patch?'

Charlie looked at her hard. She was smiling, just a little curl at the corner of her mouth. Here was a turn up for the books, no mistake. *Stretch's bird, practically propositioning him!* He'd never even thought he stood a chance with her.

'Think it over for a minute,' Letitia said, turning away from the bar. 'I'm goin' to the girls' room.'

Charlie watched her go, her hips swaying, the pantie-line sharp and clear through the tight fabric of her trousers. *Bloody hell!*

He ordered two more drinks and thought carefully. Was this his lucky day or wasn't it? He'd opened a car door, looked in and there it was, down on the floor by the pedals. A wallet. His heart had started to thump, even while he was telling himself it was probably empty. He had scored on his first car of the evening. It was a sign, nothing less. And now this. Stretch's sexy big girlfriend, asking him to take her out for the evening. *Asking* him! When fortune smiled on a bloke, Charlie reckoned he was mad to turn his back on it. Worse than mad.

An hour later they were in the lounge bar of an Islington pub called Rusty's. Charlie's sense of his own good fortune had demanded that he top-up at a higher speed than usual. He wasn't drunk but his tongue was loose enough to let some floodgates slide open. Letitia, dreamy-eyed on five drinks, regarded Charlie with the awed respect of a teenager in the presence of an idol. She had looked that way since she saw the size of the wad he was carrying.

'I've always felt lucky,' Charlie said, swirling his drink. He had switched from pints to shorts. His whisky had a lot of ginger ale in it, but he had a beer drinker's gulp and still managed to sink most of the glassful in two swallows. 'I've not always had luck workin' for me, but it's been there all the time. Lurkin'. Lately it's stepped forward, this lucky streak. An' it's out in the open for keeps. I can tell.'

'I've not been on a date with a really lucky fella before,' Letitia told him. 'I've thought I was sometimes, but it never worked out that way. You know how it goes – some flash git asks you out for a noggin an' a bite to eat, an' you think, this is all right, here's a bloke with a bit of gelt an' some style on him. A winner. Then it all comes out. He's up to his arse in debts an' just takin' you out to get his mind off things for a couple of hours. Except he doesn't get his mind off anythin', an' all he does is tell you about it. You get the lot – his hard luck, his troubles with the wife an' kids, the shit the world's dropped on him, all that.' She moved closer to Charlie on the velour-covered seat, letting her hip nudge him softly. 'I know Stretch comes on heavy, like he's some kind of big-time operator, but he's small stuff really. Twenty-six an' still livin' with his mum. Pickin' up dole money an' doin' dodgy jobs on the side. A born loser if you ask me.' She touched Charlie's sleeve. 'I could always see you were a bit different. You've got somethin' about you a girl can spot.' She narrowed her eyes. 'You've just been usin' Stretch, haven't you?'

Charlie made a wavy gesture with his hand, a maybe-yes, maybe-no sign. 'I'm just careful with people,' he said. 'I have to be. It can get lonely, mind. Not bein' able to open right up, not able to risk makin' real friends.'

Letitia nodded. 'I think I know what you mean. It's hard to trust people. A girl knows that more than most.'

'Yeah.' Charlie had the feeling he was floating. Nothing could go wrong, he was sailing on eighteen-carat good fortune. He had already begun to figure out where he would take Letitia for the big scene. 'I hope you don't think you can't trust me, though,' he said, giving Letitia his steady-eyed stare, the look Judy said made her feel funny right down to her heels.

'I wouldn't be here if I thought you wasn't straight, would I?'

'True enough.'

'I'll tell you somethin', Charlie Cotton.' It was necessary for Letitia to look coy. She did it by putting her head down until her chin was nearly touching her chest, then rolling her eyes back to look up at Charlie. 'I've fancied you since the first time I saw you.'

His ears singing, Charlie said, 'I thought you didn't rate me much.'

'I had to keep up appearances, hadn't I?'

Charlie nodded. 'I can see that, yeah.' He reached to his hip pocket and flashed out the money again. 'Let's get you another drinkie.'

'Ta.'

At the bar Charlie took stock. Here he was, safely out of the searchlight in a snug little pub in Islington, getting all lined up with a tasty bit of skirt. Tonight was a certainty, but what about later? When a bloke got himself set up with another bloke's woman, and the other bloke happened to be a pal, the odds were the set-up would get discovered in double quick time. And Stretch was a vindictive man with some unpleasant connections in the muscle department. Charlie was confident enough that his luck made him bomb-proof, but there was nothing wrong in a bit of caution. He would have to check up on Letitia's view of the future and see if they could work something out.

He came back with the fresh drinks and sat down. Letitia had lit up a cigarette and was blowing nervy little plumes to right and left. 'I get a bit jumpy stayin' one place too long,' she said, reaching for her glass. 'Fancy goin' somewhere else when we've finished?'

Charlie said that was a good idea. 'Any place special?'

'How about your place?'

He stared at her. 'I'm in a kind of difficult situation, when it comes to takin' anybody home . . .'

Letitia nodded. 'I know. You're married. What I meant was, if you want to get yourself a place for the night, I don't mind sharin' it with you.'

Fleetingly Charlie wondered how many times she had done this before. 'A hotel room, you mean?'

'Yeah.' Her expression now was confident, unhesitant. An understanding had been reached. There was no more need for coyness. 'There's one or two places round here. Or we could go for somethin' fancier, if you like.'

Charlie thought of the wad. He could easily afford a room in a good hotel and hardly notice the dent it left in his capital. 'Tell you what,' he said. 'We'll go an' get a bite to eat when we leave here. Then I'll find us a nice place where we can get to know each other better. How does that sound to you?'

'Great.'

That was that, Charlie thought. All arranged. No obstacles. But the question of future events was still nagging. 'Listen, Letitia, we're goin' to have to talk about how we organize ourselves. I mean, I like you a lot an' I think you feel the same way about me, so this isn't just

96

for tonight, is it? What with me knowin' Stretch, though, an' you sort of bein' his regular girlfriend . . .'

'No problem,' Letitia said, edging close again. 'Stretch knows as much as I want him to know.'

'Yeah, but even so, he's pretty sharp, love. He catches on fast. I don't fancy gettin' my ears razored off or nothin' like that.'

Letitia leaned so close Charlie felt her breath on his cheek. 'Listen. If Stretch knew the half of it, he'd have left marks all over me long ago, not to mention one or two of his so-called pals.'

Charlie didn't think he wanted to go into the details of that. For one thing, it meant facing the fact that Letitia, for all her style and sex-appeal, had the kind of history that got girls labelled Tart, Slag or Pop-On. He sat there looking at his drink, feeling safety close round him. It would be all right. He could have a fling with Letitia – a long-term arrangement, if his luck lived up to its promises – and there would be no trouble.

'Drink up, Letitia. I'm really ready for a bit of the old curry now.'

'Me too,' she said, giving his knee a bold, firm squeeze. 'But I'm leavin' room for my afters.'

Charlie got back to Walford at ten past nine the next morning. He called at a café for a cup of tea before he went home. What he really needed, he believed, was a shot of pain-killer, morphine or something as strong. He felt terrible. And at the same time he felt marvellous. He had spent the kind of night which, if he had read about it in a blue book when he was a kid, would have kept him awake for a week, just picturing it.

His memory offered no proper chronology of events. They had eaten and afterwards they had taken a taxi to the Bayswater Road, where Letitia knew a nice hotel. They booked a double room. Letitia said she fancied a drink before they turned in, so they went to the bar, which was small and suitably hushed, a plush enclosure where couples huddled clandestinely in corners and spoke in whispers. After a couple of drinks they went to their room, taking with them a bottle of Asti Spumanti and two glasses. From that point on, Charlie's recollection was a feverish jumble.

Letitia, he believed, had something wrong with her mind, but he would be prepared to fight tooth and claw to stop anybody correcting the defect. She had drained him. In the process she had shifted his view of himself and the kind of life he wanted to live. The shift was only slight but it was monumental; from hesitant craving he had moved into the area of positively wanting, whatever the cost. This was the life for Charlie – fast women, access to the world of realized fantasy, and money. He couldn't imagine anything else mattering to him any more. The only change he would make, next time he had a scene with Letitia or whoever, would be to forget the Asti, especially if they'd had curry first. His head felt like it was going to burst.

He got back to the house at twenty to ten. An instant before he let himself into their room he knew it was empty. He didn't know how he sensed that, but he was right. There was a note on the mantelpiece, written in heavy capitals:

GONE TO THE HOSPITAL.
THE PAINS HAVE STARTED.

Charlie stood staring at the window for a minute. Domestic reality was like a knife in his heart. Dot was in the hospital, therefore he had to go there. Duty called.

'Christ . . .'

He had just spent the night with a woman who'd taken him to the delicious gates of hell; she was the perfect embodiment of his most overheated dreams, an avaricious sensualist with whom he could do what he liked. Dot, the woman who made him feel like cutting his throat at times, the woman who kept him on the frozen wasteland at his own side of the bed, who didn't have one spontaneous emotional gesture in her, and with whom he couldn't do one thing he liked, was about to imprison him in fatherhood – *and it was his duty to consider her above all others*. They were married, after all.

When he got to the hospital he was told that Dot was asleep. There had been complications during the delivery; Dot was rather poorly, but the baby was fine. It was a boy.

Charlie sat in the waiting room, smoking, lighting one cigarette off the end of another. A decision was forming, hardening to the point where he could begin to act on it. He thought of Dot every few minutes, checking his conscience, and felt no guilt. Once or twice he thought of his son and felt nothing.

'Sod it. Sod the lot of it.'

He had luck on his side now and he had found a mode of existence that he wanted. All former dreams and delusions were cancelled. Charlie Cotton had located his path, it was the way he wanted – and needed. There would be some awkwardness, some pain for Dot, but whatever the cost, he wasn't going to settle further into the cold mud of his marriage. Bugger the cost, he thought. The things he wanted were worth a little suffering.

10

Time was like an accordion, Dot believed. Sometimes it stretched ahead of her, its endless pleats unfolding, a wearying mileage of ups and downs that had to be covered, whether she was fit for the trip or not. Then the accordion would close; an event that seemed only a month or two in the past turned out to have been a year or more ago, and future events would rush at her, catching her unaware, unprepared.

Young Nick's seventh birthday seemed to arrive years too soon. Babyhood had had its endless times – long nights when he had been teething, others when he cried hour after hour for no apparent reason; when he'd had measles Dot thought it would go on forever. But even so, seven came too fast. Her baby boy was no longer a baby, he hadn't been for years. That was hard to believe, too.

She had seen him off to school that morning with the promise that he'd have a slap-up party when he got home. He'd looked at her dully and said he didn't think he wanted a party. 'Of course you do,' Dot told him, ruffling his hair. 'You'll have sandwiches and cakes and jelly and you can play games with your little friends.' Nick made a face and walked away across the playground. He didn't look back, not even when Dot called to him and waved.

'What did you get him for his birthday, then?' Mrs Courtney asked when Dot got to work.

'A little electric train set. Got it through the club. The man next door had to put a plug on it for me.'

'Was Nick pleased with it?'

Dot's mouth twitched, the way it usually did when she was uncertain about something. 'He'd only had it out of the box five minutes before he broke it. I'll have to get it seen to.'

'Kids can be so destructive,' Mrs Courtney murmured, putting on her overall.

'I'm sure Nick didn't do it deliberately,' Dot said sharply. People had noticed she was fiercely defensive where her son was concerned. 'The thing was just a bit flimsy, that's all. Nothin's built to last nowadays.'

'This vacuum cleaner certainly wasn't.' Mrs Courtney hauled the battered and patched cylinder cleaner out of the broom cupboard and began dragging it along the corridor. Dot followed, carrying a mop and bucket. The two women worked together five days a week at the Walford Borough Council offices, cleaning and taking turns at being tea lady. Mrs Courtney was twenty-nine, the same age as Dot, but she had the manner of a much older woman. She kept making remarks like 'when I was young' and 'young people don't understand'. On the whole Dot liked her. She was cheerful company, never got flustered and was always a soothing influence when things got on top of Dot.

They started in the County Clerk's office. He was always out on Thursdays and that gave them time to do a thorough job. Dot did the dusting while Mrs Courtney hoovered the floor. The work was automatic, carried out with the absentness of a habit.

'Did Nick get anythin' from his dad?' Mrs Courtney asked over the hum of the cleaner.

'A card,' Dot said, frowning at the table she was polishing.

'Anythin' in it?'

'His love an' best wishes.'

Mrs Courtney made no comment. She knew, as a lot of people did, that Charlie Cotton was a waster, and that he had left Dot years ago. He had started drifting away from her soon after the boy was born. The absences got longer

101

and longer, until he finally stayed away. He lived with another woman somewhere in North London. Dot had told Mrs Courtney that he came back from time to time, just to see how she and the boy were getting along. A neighbour of Dot's had said he only ever came back to scrounge off her, or to sleep on the sofa when he was between girlfriends. Nobody had ever been able to explain why a woman's man like Charlie had ever married a dry stick like Dot in the first place. They couldn't understand, either, why she had never divorced him.

'Goin' round the pub again tonight?' Mrs Courtney asked, after a decent pause to let the subject of Charlie drop.

Dot stopped polishing and looked at her. 'I hope you don't think I go round there every night.'

'Of course I don't.'

'I go round when I can get somebody to sit with Nick, which isn't very often.'

'I know you enjoy the company.'

'It's the only reason I ever go.' Dot sighed. 'It's a pity the other people just go there to drink. Or that's their main reason, anyway. I don't see why they don't just have a tomato juice like me. They'd enjoy themselves just as much.'

'Didn't you ever take a drink, then?'

'No. I avoid poisons.'

Mrs Courtney shrugged. 'I must say I enjoy the odd port an' lemon. Even a brandy, now an' then.'

They were interrupted by Mr Logan, the tall, dour-faced staff supervisor. 'Could I have a word, Mrs Cotton? In my office, please.'

Dot dropped her duster and stared at Mrs Courtney. It terrified her when Mr Logan spoke to her. He reminded her of a teacher she'd once had at school, a man who kept threatening to cane her for her stupidity.

'Go ahead, love,' Mrs Courtney said as Logan stepped back out into the corridor. 'He won't eat you.'

'But what's he want?' Dot tucked a strand of hair into her turban and nervously fingered the buttons of her overall. 'I wasn't late or nothin', was I?'

'Course you wasn't. You'll find out soon enough what it is. Don't keep him waitin'. You know what he's like.'

Logan was already sitting behind the desk when Dot got to his office. She flashed her teeth at him, wondering whether she should sit down or remain standing by the filing cabinet.

'How long have you worked here, Mrs Cotton?' Logan's hands were folded on the desk. That was something else Dot remembered about that teacher, all those years ago. He always composed his hands carefully before he threatened her. 'Two years, is it?'

'Two an' a bit.'

Logan nodded. 'So you've known the rules for long enough, haven't you? I mean it's not as if you wouldn't, after all this time. You know exactly what your job is. You are employed to clean these offices and to make and serve tea to council employees working here.'

'Yes, that's right . . .' Dot's mind was racing. Was he saying she wasn't doing her job right? Had somebody been complaining about her dusting and polishing, or the way she swabbed the corridors?

'And just as there are things you're required to do,' Logan continued, 'there are things you mustn't do.'

'Yes, well, I'm sure I stick to the rules, Mr Logan . . .' Dot couldn't hold his eyes. They were stern, penetrating.

Logan opened his desk and took out a folded sheet of yellow paper with a picture printed on it. 'Are you saying you didn't put this up on the clerical staff notice board?'

Dot squinted at the paper. For a moment she didn't recognize it, then she realized what it was. 'Well, I didn't see no harm in it. Just the opposite, in fact.'

'It's not a question of good or harm. You've no right whatever to pass on personal messages or personal points of view via the official notice boards in this building.'

'It's the Lord's message,' Dot said. 'I was doin' my Christian duty an' nothin' more.' She was surprising herself. She'd never thought she could defend herself this strongly to the likes of Mr Logan. But that was how God worked. He gave courage to those who spoke on his behalf. 'I tacked it over that terrible picture somebody had stuck on the board. Like I said, it was my duty as a Christian.'

Logan held up the paper. 'This is a tract on lewdness and depravity, from what I can gather. You attached it to a poster advertising an evening study course on Impressionist painting. Why did you do that?'

'That's an indecent picture on that poster, Mr Logan. Have you seen it? It's scandalous.'

'Listen to me, Mrs Cotton. That indecent picture, as you call it, is a brilliant and very famous work of art.'

Dot felt her indignation rise. 'I can't see anythin' brilliant in a picture of a naked woman washin' herself, if that's what she's doin'.'

'It's a nude, I'll grant you that.' Logan sighed. 'A nude by Renoir.'

'Another mucky Frenchman, by the sound of him.'

'Now that'll do, Mrs Cotton,' Logan warned.

'I have to speak my mind –'

'Not on that notice board, you won't.' Logan dropped the tract on the desk. 'If you ever do anything of this kind again, you'll find yourself in grave danger of dismissal.'

Dot clamped her mouth shut and stared at the floor.

'Have I made myself clear?'

Dot nodded.

'Very well. You can get back to your work now.'

Mrs Courtney was moving the vacuum cleaner back into the corridor when Dot came back.

'Well? What was it all about?'

'It was about sinfulness bein' allowed to run rampant through this place without bein' hindered.' Dot stamped into the County Clerk's office and came out again with her dusters. 'It was about indecency bein' advertised an' the Lord's message gettin' scorned an' cast aside.' She clamped a hand to her forehead. 'Lord, I need a cup of tea.'

They had a break at half-past ten. Dot sat by the table in the little basement kitchen, puffing a cigarette and watching Mrs Courtney make the tea.

'How long have you been smokin'?' Mrs Courtney asked. 'I don't remember seein' you with a fag before.'

'I only have one when my nerves is bad,' Dot said.

She had no clear recollection of when she had started. It was one night when she was in a jittery mood and she'd found a packet with two in it that Charlie had left behind after one of his fleeting visits. She had heard often enough that smoking was good for the nerves. The first few puffs had made her dizzy and she coughed a lot. But somehow it had become a habit. And she reasoned it couldn't be a sin, because the new minister smoked and so did his wife.

'You shouldn't let people upset you so easily,' Mrs Courtney said. 'You've been shakin' like an aspen since Logan spoke to you.'

'I don't choose to let people upset me,' Dot pointed out. 'They just do. It happens, I can't control it.'

'What you need's a holiday.' Mrs Courtney put a mug of tea in front of Dot and watched her spoon in the sugar. 'A good rest would be just the ticket.'

'Where would I get the money for a holiday? It's a struggle keepin' Nick an' myself clothed an' fed, let alone anythin' else.'

'Well, it's a scrapin' job for us too, but we always

manage to get a week away somewhere. You've got to break the year up.'

'As far as I'm concerned,' Dot said, 'they can break this one up an' chuck it away. It's been terrible so far, an' it's not halfway over yet.'

She believed firmly that God handed out individual punishments, as well as the larger-scale affairs that he visited on whole countries and continents. This year the Lord had either been busier than usual, or He had lost control. The world seemed to be in chaos. There was news of famine, drought, wars, murder and mayhem. America had been swept by tornadoes. There was a huge cyclone in Pakistan. If all that wasn't God's wrath, Dot had no idea what was. She hardly dared switch on her little TV set when the news was on, for fear of what she might see and hear. And there had been so many sad deaths; Winston Churchill had gone to his rest, so had Nat 'King' Cole, Albert Schweitzer, Somerset Maugham and somebody called T. S. Eliot – Dot believed he was an old-time music hall entertainer, though she wasn't sure.

British youth had gone barmy, although that was a process that had started a long time ago. When it wasn't sex and drink they were spending their time and money on, it was pop music. The Beatles' so-called tunes blared from every radio and record player, from every jukebox in every café and pub. It wasn't just the Beatles; there were other screeching hairies with names like The Kinks, The Rolling Stones, Herman's Hermits, The Animals, The Byrds and dozens of others. They were no better than the benighted heathen black man, muttering his mumbo-jumbo in his clay hut. It was one of Dot's few certainties that she would protect her Nick from all the evils that lay in ambush to trap innocent children. He would grow up with a proper set of principles and a decent fear of the Lord.

Two cups of tea and another cigarette had a calming effect on Dot. She began to talk about her plans for Nick's birthday party.

'He knows he's havin' one, but it's still goin' to be a surprise,' she said. 'Mrs Lovat – she's the mum of one of his little pals, lives round the corner from us – she's goin' to collect him from school an' keep him at her place so I can get things ready. I've got a whole big tin of fairy cakes, I'm makin' sandwiches with three different fillin's, an' the jelly's settin' already in the cool box. The big surprise is goin' to be the birthday cake, though. Blue an' white icin', with a big seven on it, edged with them things like ball bearings that you can eat.'

'Sounds lovely,' Mrs Courtney said. 'How many of his pals are comin'?'

'Both of them.'

'Only two?'

Dot nodded. 'I'm fussy about who he plays with, you see. I don't want him mixin' with roughs an' toughs and boys that swear. Mrs Lovat's a member of the same congregation as me, an' her boy's an absolute angel. The other lad's a quiet little soul. Got a squint. He stays in a lot an' reads.'

Mrs Courtney looked at the clock. 'Better be gettin' back to it, I suppose. Don't want Logan on our backs, do we?'

Dot stubbed out her cigarette and stood up. She rinsed out the cups. As she was drying them she said, 'You know, I'm beginnin' to get quite excited about the party.'

'Yeah, well, it should be fun for you,' Mrs Courtney said. For some people, she thought, there was precious little fun in life. Although she was a little ashamed to admit it to herself, it often made her feel more contented with her own situation, just working with someone who led such a bleak life. A kids' party, even one with only three kids at it, would probably give Dot the kind of kick some other women could only get from an orgy.

Everything was ready by half-past four. The square dining table had a white paper cover with a red and green border, and the plates of cakes and sandwiches were set out in a circle around the birthday cake, which sat at the centre. Each of the boys' places was laid with a plate, napkin, knife, fork and spoon. At the appropriate time, dishes of jelly would be brought through from the kitchen and set before the children. There was even a jug of cream.

Dot stood by the living room door, hands clasped, marvelling at how the table display transformed the place. She had done what she could by way of furnishings and decoration for the house, but it rarely seemed better than drab. At the times when it started to depress her, Dot reminded herself she was lucky to have the place. It was very old and the council had skimped on renovations when they bought it; but Dot had her own front and back doors, her own bath and toilet, and separate rooms for herself and Nick to sleep in. She counted herself blessed.

'A proper picture it looks,' she murmured. She walked round the table one more time, straightening the cutlery, adjusting the position of a plate of sandwiches, then she went to the window to see if Nick was coming yet. There was no sign of him, so she decided to have another cup of tea, just to while away the time.

At ten to five there was a knock at the door. Dot hurried through from the kitchen, brushing at her freshly-ironed pinnie, preparing her smile of welcome. When she opened the door she found Mrs Martin on the step. She was the mother of the little boy with the squint. She looked apologetic.

'I'm terribly sorry, Mrs Cotton. My Daniel won't be able to come to Nick's birthday do.'

'Oh, dear. Why ever not?'

'He's got diarrhoea. Been eatin' somethin' a boy gave him at school, far as I can make out. I'm awful sorry.' She produced a little packet from her handbag. It was wrapped in coloured paper with tinsel string. 'Here's Nick's present, anyhow.'

Dot took it with both hands. 'Thanks very much. I'm sure he'll love it. He'll be very disappointed Daniel couldn't come, though.'

'Yes, well, it couldn't be helped. Perhaps next time.'

When Mrs Martin had gone Dot went back to the living room and looked at the table again. It was going to be a quiet party. She sighed and removed Daniel's place setting. She was putting the cutlery back in the kitchen drawer when the door was knocked again.

'Who can this be?' she muttered as she went to answer it. Nick would have let himself and little Paul in. She opened the door. Mrs Lovat, Paul's mother, was standing there. Nick was beside her, scowling at the ground.

'Well, hello, there,' Dot said, trying for a smile, wondering why Mrs Lovat looked so grim.

'I've brought your son back to you,' Mrs Lovat snapped. 'I'd be grateful if you saw to it, in future, that he doesn't play with my boy. Or talk to him.'

'Pardon?' Dot looked at Nick, then back at Mrs Lovat. 'Isn't Paul comin', then? To the party I mean.'

'He certainly is not. I know you're a church-goin' woman, Mrs Cotton, just like I am. That's what makes it so astonishin'.'

'What?'

'This lad's language. An' his viciousness.'

'My Nick? Usin' language?'

'Language of the likes that's never been uttered in my home since we moved in twenty years ago. Disgustin'.'

'Nick?' Dot leaned down, trying to make him look at

her, but he wouldn't. 'Is this true what Mrs Lovat's tellin' me?'

'Of course it's true,' Mrs Lovat said indignantly. 'I wouldn't say it if it wasn't true.'

Dot shook her head. She was bewildered. 'What happened, then, exactly?'

'They were playin' in the front room. I put them in there with a ludo board while I was gettin' my hubby's dinner ready. They'd only been in there five minutes an' I hear Paul screamin'. I rushes in an' this one here's got Paul by the hair an' he's banging his head on the wall. Not only that, but he was callin' him an effin' bee.'

Dot's hand flew to her mouth. 'Oh! Never!'

'So like I say, I'd be obliged if you'd keep Nick well away from Paul. If you don't, I'll talk to the Welfare people about it.' Mrs Lovat turned and strode away.

Dot took Nick by the shoulder and led him into the living room. Shaking, she sat down on the armchair and looked at him. 'Now you tell me, an' tell me now, young man – where did you pick up language like that?'

Nick glared at her. Every day she saw his father in that face. 'I didn't say nothin'. She was makin' it up.'

'Nick! You mustn't tell lies!'

'It's that old fat cow that's lyin'!'

'*Nick!*'

'Well she is!'

'Go to your room straight away! This very minute! You can come out when you're ready to tell me the truth!'

He narrowed his eyes at her and looked as if he was going to say something else. Then he turned and ran through to his bedroom.

Dot stared across at the table. After all that expectation – the laughter of the children, the cleared plates, the games afterwards . . .

She wiped away a tear with a corner of her pinnie. It

was boys at school who were corrupting Nick, of course. It had to be that. Whenever he was anywhere out of her sight, he would be at risk. The poor lad, she thought. What chance did he stand?

She stood up. Maybe she would be able to coax him to sit at the table with her, later, when she'd given him a little telling-off and then said they were friends again. They could have a party on their own, her and Nick. She would see to it that his day wasn't completely spoiled. Whatever he'd done, she owed that to him. Who else did the little lad have but his mum? And who else had she?

Suddenly Dot was missing Charlie terribly. She clutched the edge of the table, trying not to cry.

11

Towards the end of the year there was an event which amounted, in the language of Dot's minister, to nothing less than an epiphany. Mr Whitehead came into Dot's life, and she found herself being transformed.

His full name was Rodney Everett Whitehead. He was tall and fine-boned, with blue eyes that reminded Dot of the colour on willow pattern plates. He was thin-lipped but smiled a lot, and his reddish brown hair was neatly parted and held in place with brilliantine. Mr Whitehead was a pharmacist by profession and a lay preacher by inclination. Dot first encountered him one Sunday evening when he was guest preacher at the chapel.

Mr Whitehead preached on the subject of loneliness. His words carried a rich understanding of his topic and his voice, deep and resonant, was full of reassurance. He sounded, to Dot at least, like a man who could be relied upon; if he said something was so, then it very likely would be so.

'Whom the heart of man shuts out,' he said that evening, 'sometimes the heart of God takes in.'

Dot memorized that. It was one of the most comforting things she had ever heard. But there was more.

'Every human being needs love. It is a birthright. True friendship is one of the richest forms of love. Even if we have only one real friend, we can never know loneliness, so it is well to remember that God is our friend, companion, guide and succour. He is everything a friend could be – and more, because he is also our Father, the designer of our fate and cherisher of our spirits.'

Mr Whitehead's eyes roamed the congregation. 'So

why is there so much loneliness in the world?' he demanded. 'Why are there such things as lonely-hearts clubs, lonely-hearts columns in newspapers and magazines, cries of anguish in shop-window advertisements from men and women seeking a friend? Why all that, plus the un-advertised sorrowing of souls behind drawn curtains, adrift on rafts of isolation, surrounded by seas of loneliness? The reason is that they do not acknowledge their truest friend. They do not trust in the friendship of God, whose hand is eternally held out to them.' Mr Whitehead raised a finger solemnly. 'Acknowledge God, and loneliness is banished. Was there ever such a simple cure for such a terrible ailment?'

By that point Dot had become very emotional. That very morning, sitting in the living room with her second cup of tea, she had looked around her and wondered that she could live with such isolation. Young Nick, from whom it was hard to draw even a smile, seemed to save whatever warmth and friendship he possessed for his solitary games in the yard, talking in excited whispers to imaginary companions. He didn't fill Dot's life the way she went on hoping he would. He never stayed in unless he was forced to, and then he would either sit sullenly in his room, or play in a corner with his toys. Dot's truest friends in the house, in her *life*, were the things around her, the objects she daily saw and touched. They were her mute companions. And by attaching herself to them, by learning loneliness in their midst, she had laid herself open to more pain than ever.

Now she was ashamed of herself, and at the same time she felt a great bolstering of her spirit. Mr Whitehead's words had reminded her that she was never alone. Not with God to talk to and share her life with. She had known it all along, of course, but a person sometimes needed reminding of just how well-off she was.

'It is a true saying,' Mr Whitehead said, 'that if you

seek a faultless friend, you will remain friendless. But it is only true if you seek such a friend among mankind. Turn to the friendship of God and you will find a companionship so flawless, so dazzling in its perfection, that your heart will forever brim with joy. You will know the deepest sense of belonging that man can achieve.'

Dot wasn't one to push herself, but as soon as the service ended she stood up and pushed her way forward, determined to speak to Mr Whitehead. She had to wait a couple of minutes, moving restlessly from foot to foot, as other members of the congregation paid their compliments and respects. Finally, when she was beside the man and he turned to her, Dot was able to blurt out her small prepared statement.

'Thank you ever so much, Mr Whitehead. That was one of the loveliest sermons I've ever sat an' listened to.'

He smiled. 'It's kind of you to say so, Mrs . . .'

'Cotton. Mrs Cotton. I'm a regular member of the congregation here. I just wanted to let you know how much I was comforted by what you said.' She took a step away from Mr Whitehead, feeling she'd said as much as she should. But he was still smiling at her, and he was doing it in a way that invited her to linger.

'If it's not impertinent of me, Mrs Cotton – when you say my sermon comforted you, am I to take it you have some recent experience of loneliness?'

'Well, yes, I suppose so.' Dot was flustered. It was unusual to have someone so well-spoken take an interest in her.

A tiny frown creased Mr Whitehead's brow. 'I notice you're here alone – widowhood wouldn't be the cause of your loneliness, would it?'

'Oh no, no. But my husband, he, well, he left me some time ago, an' there's only me an' my little boy. It gets very lonely sometimes. Of course I should have remembered the Lord is always there, but . . .'

114

'But at times our faith flounders and becomes a little weak,' Whitehead cut in smoothly. 'That's why there's always a need for the preacher, Mrs Cotton. He's there to keep faith on the rails, to remind people of the debit and credit of the religious life.'

'Yes, quite.' Dot cleared her throat. 'Well, I'll be off, then.'

'Ah, we're having coffee in the vestry, I believe,' Mr Whitehead said, pointing to where the minister and some others were clustered by the door. 'Would you care to join us?'

Two things happened at once. Dot said yes, she would love to, and she wondered if the woman sitting with Nick would mind her being late. There had been some stiffness once before when Dot missed the bus and had to walk back from chapel. Babysitters, especially cheap ones, were hard to find. She didn't want to lose this one.

'I'll have to make it quick,' she said as she followed Mr Whitehead to the door. 'My babysitter'll be upset if I'm back much later than I said I'd be.'

'How long does it take you to get home from here?'

'Well usually there's a ten minute wait for the bus, then six or seven minutes on the bus itself, an' a couple of minutes' walk to the house . . .'

'About twenty minutes, all told,' Mr Whitehead murmured. 'No problem at all, Mrs Cotton. I'll be leaving after fifteen minutes anyway. I can give you a lift. A car's quicker, so you'll most probably get home a little earlier than you're expected.'

'Oh, I couldn't take you out of your way – '

'It's no trouble, I assure you.'

Dot was overwhelmed by the man's Christian charity. 'It's awfully kind of you. Truly.'

The following ten minutes were packed with more inspiration and heart-lift than Dot had experienced in years. After chatting briefly to the others in turn, Mr

Whitehead skilfully drew Dot in from the perimeter of the gathering and seemed more and more to address his remarks directly to her.

'To flee from God is to flee into oneself,' he said, in response to a remark of the minister's. Dot tucked that one away in her memory with a few others she'd already put there that night.

'Running after happiness is running away from contentment.'

How true! Dot thought.

'It's always better to suffer an injustice than to commit one.'

It would soon be impossible to remember so much wisdom. Dot's memory had a severely limited capacity, and it tended to leak anyway. After a few minutes she decided just to let it all wash refreshingly over her, nodding and muttering her agreement, smiling her appreciation. She had truly never met a man before who carried his religious knowledge so easily. He was stylish, compared to the minister, who tended to sound unsure of himself. And Mr Whitehead gave the impression he had an answer for everything.

On the way home, sitting bolt upright in Mr Whitehead's big shiny car and feeling very regal, Dot thanked him again for the sermon, and for taking her home.

'The pleasure, both in preaching and helping people, is all mine, Mrs Cotton. I count myself fortunate to have the God-granted gift of oratory. It's brought me friends and filled my life.' After a pause he added, 'After losing my wife, I dedicated every spare moment to my religion, and to spreading its message.'

'Oh dear,' Dot said. 'Was it long ago she passed away, your wife?'

'Nine years ago. She didn't pass away, though. She ran away. So . . .' He turned his head briefly and smiled at

Dot. 'We have something in common besides our faith, haven't we?'

'Indeed we have,' Dot sighed, wondering what kind of woman would run away from a man like him.

As he drew up at the end of Dot's street Mr Whitehead handed her a little card from the shelf above the dashboard. 'That's the address of my shop – I've a chemist's on Orpington Road. My business 'phone number and my home one are at the bottom. If you ever want to talk . . .' He paused and made an apologetic smile. 'Please don't think I'm being forward. I've been through an experience similar to yours, that's all, and I've had to find some answers the hard way. There are times when it must be difficult for you to bear up on your own. I'd be happy to chat with you any time you think it might help.'

Dot was overwhelmed all over again. She took the card, nodding her thanks. After an awkward scramble to get out of the car she stood in the road and waved to Mr Whitehead through the window. He waved back, smiling warmly, and drove away.

A week passed. Dot found it was impossible to get Mr Whitehead out of her mind. If she wasn't thinking about the glorious message in his words, she was dwelling on *him*, the man, the way he carried himself, his propriety and charm. She kept hearing his voice as he told her he would gladly chat with her whenever she thought it would help.

On Saturday she decided she would take a tablet to calm her nerves, then she would 'phone him. At eleven o'clock, just as she was getting her coat on to go down to the telephone box at the end of the road, a policeman came to the door.

'Mrs Cotton?'

Dot nodded, fear clutching her heart.

'It's about your son . . .'

117

'Oh my God in heaven!' She staggered back. 'Nothin's happened to him? Tell me nothin's happened!'

'He's all right,' the policeman said. 'I mean he's not hurt or anything like that. But there's been a bit of trouble. I want you to come down to the station with me. We've got him there. The inspector wants a word with you.'

When they got to the station Dot was shown into a small, featureless interview room. She sat with her hands on the table, clicking the tips of her nails against each other, wishing she had brought her cigarettes. She couldn't imagine what was wrong. She didn't want to try imagining. A migraine was buzzing its warning at the back of her head.

After a few minutes a uniformed inspector came in. He was a red-faced, tubby man. He reminded Dot of the bobbies she used to see on the beat when she was a little girl. He nodded to her and sat down at the opposite side of the table.

'Thank you for coming, Mrs Cotton,' he said. 'I'm Inspector Cuthbert.'

'What's happenin'? Where's my Nick?'

'He's in a room across the passage with three of his pals. They're being given a good tongue-lashing. You'll be able to take him home with you.'

'What's he done? Have them other lads been gettin' up to mischief an' draggin' him into it with them? Is that what it is?'

The inspector tapped the table for a moment, watching his knuckles. 'It's not quite like that, actually. As far as I can see it's just the opposite.' He rapped the table again. 'Mrs Cotton, is it true your lad's only seven?'

She nodded. 'Eight in a few months.'

'Astonishing.'

Dot's eyes were wide with apprehension. 'What is it that's happened, then?'

'I'll come to that in a minute. Tell me something, has the lad been in any kind of trouble before?'

'No. Never.'

'How does he behave at home? I mean is he just like other kids, or is he the moody type? You know, a brooder?'

Dot's back stiffened. 'He's just a normal little boy.'

'I gather he's an only child. How about pets? Has he ever had one? A hamster, anything like that?'

'I don't hold with them, not that he's ever asked for any. They're dirty things, they spread germs.'

Now the inspector was drumming the fingers of both hands. He hunched forward and looked at Dot. 'Today, your boy stole a puppy from a pet shop on the High Road.'

'Never! I don't believe it!'

'It was in a cardboard box with the rest of its litter near the shop door. Your son sent his three pals in to ask about some tortoises in the window, and while the shop-keeper was distracted your lad took the puppy, stuck it under his jumper and left the shop.'

Dot was shaking her head. 'No. It's not true. Not my Nick – he's not that kind of boy. He's not a thief.'

'He stole that animal,' Inspector Cuthbert said firmly. 'You'll have to accept that – it's the least you'll have to accept, as it happens.'

'Have you got witnesses?' Dot demanded. 'Did people see him takin' the dog? Or is it the other lads gangin' up on him, makin' him a scapegoat for somethin' they done?'

'The three other boys have been questioned individu-ally. Their stories are identical. It was one of them who reported your son, as a matter of fact. He got frightened – terrified, in fact – and he came running to the station on his own.'

'Terrified?' Dot's features were clenched, puzzled. 'What do you mean? What was he terrified about? It's not as if they'd robbed a bank or anythin'. Sounds more like a prank to me. I don't know what all the fuss is about . . .'

'The fuss, Mrs Cotton, is about what your son did to that puppy.' The inspector's mouth tightened with disgust. 'Accompanied by the three other boys, he took the animal to an area of waste ground near the railway embankment. He'd obviously been there before, because he knew where there was a can of petrol. Two of the boys held the helpless creature while your son poured fuel over it – that was when one of the lads came running to us.'

'I don't believe this!' Dot squealed. 'It's vicious lies! He's only a little boy!'

'Little boy or not, he did it. You may have noticed your kitchen matches were missing this morning.'

Dot gulped. She had searched high and low for the matches and finally had to light the gas with a piece of paper lit from the water-heater pilot light.

'Your boy put the petrol-soaked animal on the ground and set fire to it. He and his two little companions watched it run about in agony, a living torch, until its heart gave out.'

'*No!*' Dot screamed it against her hand. 'My God, no!'

'Yes, Mrs Cotton. It happened. And seven-year-old Nick Cotton did it.' The inspector looked across at the window and stared at the rooftops. 'We want a psychologist to talk to him – we need your agreement, although I think we can force the matter if we have to. The police doctor is speechless. The boy's warped, in his view, but Doctor Young's not properly qualified to go on record to that effect. It needs the evidence of an expert.'

Tears were spilling down Dot's cheeks. 'What'll they do to him?'

'It depends what the psychologist says. He's too young to be prosecuted. But there are other steps that can be taken, for the protection of man and beast, so to speak, if it's thought necessary. What I'd like to do – and this is strictly off the record, of course – is put the little bugger over my knee and tan his arse till his nose bleeds.' The inspector stood up. 'If you hang on, somebody'll bring him along to you. Later on, I'll get a policewoman to come round and talk to you about home conditions and all the other guff we'll need for our report.'

He went out. Dot found a handkerchief and dabbed her eyes. Tears, tears, tears. That was her whole life. Grief and pain, loss and hurt. For a moment she let her mind slip past her concern for Nick. She pictured a tiny dog dashing across waste land, yelping pitifully, its body engulfed in flame. The clarity of the picture startled her. She shot to her feet, gasping.

That's not what happened! They've made it up!

She went to the window, feeling suddenly claustrophobic. She gazed down at the yard behind the station, imagining she was there, instead of shut up in a little room with bare walls and a smell of carbolic. The migraine came sliding forward, a sheet of pain, connecting with her stomach and making her feel sick.

'God, what's to become of us?'

She watched her breath put a damp cloud on the glass. The yearning that came at every moment of pain or crisis rose in her now. She needed something to hold to, some*one*.

Dot turned sharply from the window, transfixed on another shock. This time it hadn't been Charlie she'd ached for. More than anything, she wanted Mr Whitehead to be there.

12

On Christmas Eve Charlie Cotton invested his last thirty
shillings in a box of chocolates, a cap-firing six-shooter
and a big sheet of wrapping paper printed with holly and
robins. He wrapped the presents then walked the three
miles from his digs to Dot's place in Walford. He had his
smile ready as Dot opened the door.

'Merry Christmas,' he said, trying to make it sound
wistful as well as sincere.

Dot blinked at him. Her mouth was trying to smile,
but her eyes showed shock and confusion. 'Well. This is a
surprise . . .'

'Do I get invited in out of the cold?'

'Oh. Yes. Sorry. Come in.'

Nick was kneeling by the fireside, dismantling a battered toy bus. He looked up as his father came in, then
looked away again sharply and continued pulling off a
mudguard.

'My, you're gettin' to be a big lad,' Charlie said. He
turned to Dot when the boy didn't respond. 'I think he's
a bit shy of me.'

'He's always that way with strangers,' Dot said. She
was standing by the sofa, her fingers nervously stroking
the moquette. 'I was just about to get the tea ready. Will
you be stoppin'?'

Charlie put his parcels on the table. 'Well, if it's no
trouble – if I'm not puttin' you out, I mean . . .'

'No, no, I've enough in.' Dot pushed back an imaginary
strand of hair. 'Do you want to sit down, then, while I
get things sorted out in the kitchen?'

Charlie glanced at Nick dubiously. 'I'll come out an'

give you a hand.' He picked up the parcels again and made some show of placing them under the tinsel tree on the sideboard. 'A little Christmas something for you both.'

'Oh. Ta.'

Charlie followed Dot into the kitchen, feeling Nick's eyes on his back. 'It's nice to see you lookin' so well. Is that a new hairdo?'

Dot clattered some plates on to the work top. 'Just a perm I had done,' she said. 'Since it's the season of goodwill an' that. Always like to get my hair done for Christmas.'

'You was always a smart looker.' Charlie smiled at her warmly but she wasn't looking. She was having trouble co-ordinating her hands to the task of gathering cutlery from the drawer. 'I've been thinkin' a lot about you lately, Dot. You an' the boy.' Charlie sighed. 'Things can't have been easy for you.'

'No. Well . . .'

'God knows it ain't been sunshine an' roses for me, either.'

'Got a job, have you?'

'If you can call it that. I'm still driving a truck – for buttons. Been with this lot for a couple of months.'

'It's somethin', though. A job of work, a wage.' Dot looked at Charlie fleetingly. 'Where are you livin'?'

'I've got a little room in an old woman's house in Islington. It's all right, but she's always complainin'. Doesn't like me havin' visitors, or comin' in late, or playin' the wireless loud.' Charlie cleared his throat. 'It's my livin' arrangements I wanted to talk to you about, as a matter of fact – of course I wanted to see you an' Nick anyway, but this thing about my room's come up . . .'

Dot's face turned wary. She had heard this approach before.

'The thing is, I'm tryin' to get myself fixed up with

work in Walford again. You know, look up a few old faces, see if there's any jobs goin'. I believe old Tubby's doin' real well nowadays. He was always willin' to help out in the past. If I could just get a decent job, you see, I could get myself straightened out.'

Dot nodded. 'An' what would you do then?'

He shrugged evasively. 'It'd all have to be planned. Carefully. I wouldn't rush into anythin'.'

It was his way of saying he wouldn't be coming back to Dot. The hope she had carried all these years was not so strong now as it had once been, but there was still some pain in knowing Charlie had no plans to become a part of her life again.

'An' what's your room got to do with it?'

'It's too inconvenient, Dot. All the way over there, when it's here I want to be, in Walford – I mean the travellin' back an' forward while I'm tryin' to get myself a job. An' the expense of it. It costs a bit on the bus nowadays. On the tube, too, for that matter.'

Dot ripped the end off a packet of fish fingers. 'So what exactly did you want to talk to me about?'

'I thought, well, I wondered if you wouldn't mind me dossin' down on the couch for a few nights, just until I get myself sorted out.'

Dot picked up the frying pan and stood frowning at it. 'I'm not sure, Charlie. Things have changed a bit, you see.'

Now Charlie was frowning. 'What d'you mean?'

How could she tell him in a way he wouldn't misunderstand? Did she really understand it herself? 'I've got a friend comes round quite a bit nowadays. It would be a bit awkward . . .'

'I wouldn't be in the way, Dot. I'd stay out of the road until late. She wouldn't know I was about the place, if you didn't want her to.'

'It's not a woman friend, Charlie.'

'What are you talkin' about?'

'My friend's not a woman.'

Charlie picked up the fish-finger packet, looked at it and put it down again. He looked at Dot. 'Are you tellin' me you're seein' another bloke?'

'No. Well not the way you mean it. My friend's a man, yes, he's a gentleman whose . . .' Dot cast about for the words. 'Whose domestic situation's very much like mine. An' he's a Christian, so we have a lot in common there, too. We talk about our faith an' things like that . . .'

Charlie looked very displeased. 'How long's this been goin' on?'

'Nothin's *goin' on*, as you put it. He's been visitin' me for a bit more than a month, I suppose. He's a comfort to me, Charlie. A true friend.'

'I'll bet.'

Dot banged down the frying pan on the cooker and jumped, not meaning to make such a noise. 'I hope you're not goin' to start accusin' me of things, Charlie. I've been lookin' forward to a pleasant, peaceful Christmas. A really nice one, for a change. I don't want you nor nobody else spoilin' it.'

'All right, all right . . .' Charlie waved a placating hand. Dot's head was starting to wobble the way it did when she became agitated. 'It just come as a bit of a shock, that's all. I don't suppose it's my place to criticize, in the circumstances.'

'I told you, there's nothin' to criticize. My friend's a perfect gentleman – an' you know I'm not the sort to get up to any hanky-panky.'

'Right, sure, I'm sorry. I won't say another word about it.'

'I should hope not.'

Dot lit the gas and scooped a blob of cooking fat into the frying pan. 'How many fish fingers can you eat?'

'As many as you can spare.' Charlie stood by the

door, watching, tapping his foot. 'About usin' the couch, Dot – '

'Oh, I really don't know about that . . .'

'I promise I wouldn't show my face, except at bedtime. An' I'd be off early in the mornin's. It wouldn't be for long, anyway.'

Dot sighed. 'It's not that I'm uncharitable, Charlie,' she began, then turned and saw his hangdog face. 'Oh, what's the use.' She sighed again. 'Use the couch if you want.'

'You're a gem, Dot.' Charlie stepped close and startled her with a peck on the cheek. He stepped away again, rubbing his hands, getting ready to change the subject smartly, as he had always done whenever he got his way over something. 'The lad's very quiet, isn't he?' Charlie poked his head into the living room. 'All right there, young Nick?'

The boy didn't look up. He had reduced the bus to a pile of scrap.

Charlie turned to Dot again. 'How's he doin' at school?'

'All right,' Dot said. 'As far as I know, anyway. He'd a bit of trouble a while back – some mischief with some other boys, an' now I have to take him once a week to see a remed-remedial person.'

'What's one of them when it's at home?'

'She's a woman that talks to Nick an' asks him questions. It's all to do with changin' his behaviour.'

'Sounds dodgy,' Charlie said.

'There's nothin' wrong with him,' Dot snapped. 'People just like makin' a fuss.'

'Mm. I suppose you're right. Still, he always was a bit of a moody kid, wasn't he?'

'How would you know that?'

Charlie dug his hands into his pockets and leaned on the wall. 'I said the wrong thing again,' he murmured. 'Sorry.'

After tea, Charlie said he would have to go back to Islington to pay off his landlady and pick up his things. He would be back, he said, some time around midnight. He left Dot and Nick still sitting at the table.

He didn't go to Islington. He went to a side-street Walford pub called The Rumbold. A woman waved from a corner seat as Charlie came in. He went straight across and sat down beside her.

'Wotcher, Lynn. Been waitin' long?'

She pointed to the one inch gap between the rim of her glass and the lager froth. 'That long.'

'My timin's gettin' better.'

'Like your luck.' The woman put her elbow on the table, leaning close so that she could whisper. 'Did you get fixed up?'

Charlie nodded. 'No trouble at all. Did you bring my case?'

'It's by your feet. Of course I did the obvious, didn't I? Packed it right under everythin' else in the van.'

Charlie drew back, examining her. 'You're lookin' good,' he said.

'I'm glad you think so.' She was about thirty with a broad, over made-up face and tight-curled brown hair. She wore a black leather coat and a canary yellow polo-necked sweater. 'I suppose all this flattery's so I'll buy you a drink.'

'I'll admit I'm boracic. A pint would go down a treat.'

When they both had fresh drinks Charlie looked about him carefully, seeing no familiar faces. 'You're sure nobody in Walford knows you?' he said.

'That's why I'm here an' not in Walthamstow or Hackney or Islington, isn't it?' Lynn gave Charlie's hand a squeeze. 'Don't worry. Nobody knows me, nobody but old Liz, an' this is the last place Sid'll think of lookin' for me – if he ever *does* look for me.'

'What – you take off an' leave him, with five hundred

quid of his money in your bag, an' you reckon he won't be huntin' for you? I should think he'll be out with the bloodhounds when he discovers you've legged it.'

'He might just decide he's got off light – you know the way he adores me.'

'Yeah.' Charlie grinned. 'Like a bull fancies a red rag.'

He could still hardly believe this had happened. Lynn was the wife of a butcher in Hackney. Charlie had chatted her up when he met her with some other women at a hen party in a pub. One thing led to another, as it usually did when Charlie aimed himself at a girl. In this case he'd had extra incentive. Lynn had savings, she'd talked about them the very first night he had met her – 'I'm not like some women,' she'd said, 'tied to a man because he holds the purse strings. I've salted cash away since we got married. I've got independence.' As time passed and Charlie began seeing Lynn regularly in secret, he'd learned she wasn't just bored and restless, like a lot of wives he met. This one wanted out. So they planned an elopement.

Walford was an ideal place to go, because it was a patch Charlie knew, and nobody there knew Lynn, except her old school friend Liz, who apparently hated the butcher and would do anything for Lynn. Charlie had said that the period just after Christmas was a good time to make the move, because a lot of people left their rented flats then. 'An emotional time of year,' he'd told her. 'People split up, or go back to their roots – whatever the reasons, there's always plenty of flats for rent by the New Year. We'll be set up in no time.'

Lynn had decided she couldn't live through another Christmas with Sid. 'Him an' his bloody relatives, all sittin' round the festive table gettin' fatter an' drunker. I couldn't bear even one more dose of that.'

Christmas Eve was the earliest date she could make it, because that day her husband would go straight from the shop to his mother's, as he did most years, to give her her presents and get maudlin drunk with the old lady. It would give Lynn the necessary time to get her things packed into a little rented van and leave. Then she and Charlie would hang around Walford, she at her friend's house, he at Dot's – although he'd said nothing about it being Dot's, in fact he had never mentioned Dot's existence.

So far, everything had gone according to plan. Lynn had turned down Charlie's offer to help with loading the van – he might be seen, she pointed out, and connections might be made. Best to go to Walford by their separate routes and meet up at a pre-arranged venue. Which they had now done.

'When does your mate reckon you'll be able to start in the new job?' Lynn asked.

'In the New Year some time,' Charlie said. 'It'll really be like the old days, workin' in Walford again.'

He was sure he could find a job somewhere in the district. In the meantime, Lynn had given her unprompted promise that she would see to their finances until he was earning again. She had even taken five hundred pounds that Sid kept in a drawer at home for business emergencies. In Charlie's estimation, that money plus whatever she had in her savings account must add up to a very tidy sum. It promised to be quite a Christmas. Quite a New Year, come to that.

'Cop for this,' Lynn said, slipping him a wad of notes under the table. 'There's fifty there. That'll tide you for now, for expenses an' such.' She tapped her empty glass. 'It means you can get us a drink in, too.'

Charlie picked up the glasses. 'Lynn, you know how I hate this, about the money I mean . . .'

'Look,' she said firmly, 'we've been all through that. After what the Tax did to you, you need all the help you can get.' The story she had swallowed was that the Inland

129

Revenue had cleaned Charlie out, after making a careful search of his old tax records. He had packed in his job, he said, so they couldn't get their hands on any more. In future he would work on a strictly cash-in-hand basis. 'Just get up to that bar and get us another drinkie.'

A few minutes after eleven, as Charlie and Lynn were finishing off a Chicken Vindaloo with a side order of vegetable curry, Dot was fetching Mr Whitehead's coat. Nowadays she called him Rodney, and he called her by her first name, too. Beyond that small intimacy, all the social proprieties were observed. They both preferred it that way.

'It's been a lovely evening, Dot,' Rodney said as he slipped on his overcoat. 'It always is, I must say.'

'I've enjoyed it too,' Dot assured him.

'And you'll be at my place at two prompt tomorrow, won't you? You and young Nick.'

'Yes, we will, and it's very good of you.'

'Nonsense. It's selfish of me, to be truthful. Making sure I've got company on Christmas Day.'

Dot followed him to the door. 'You're sure you don't want me to give you a hand with the cooking?' she said. 'It'd be no trouble.'

'Not at all.' Rodney paused with his hand on the door knob. 'I'm a fairly good cook, if I do say so, and I enjoy doing it. Apart from that, I want you to have at least one day in the year when you don't have to lift a finger.' He opened the door and stepped outside.

Dot came forward and they shook hands briefly. 'See you tomorrow then, Rodney.'

'See you soon, Dot. Good night.'

'Safe home, now.'

Dot watched him get into his car and drive off, then she closed the door, went to the kitchen and poured the last cup of tea from the pot. She stood by the sink with it, thinking over the evening, smiling to herself.

They had talked about hope. Rodney always seemed to bring a theme with him, and when he had sat down by the fire tonight, almost the first thing he had said was, 'If it weren't for hope, the heart would break.' He had smiled as he said it, so Dot knew they wouldn't be talking about sad things, in spite of his words. The gist of it all, as they chatted on, was that man was kept alive by hope. 'We all hope for something better, Dot, and the promise contained at the heart of a hope, however wild, is the sustaining force. Hope steadies us. It's one of God's greatest gifts, I often think.'

It was at that point Dot had thought of Charlie. Apart from wondering if she should tell Rodney that he was back, she wondered, too, about the special hope she had cherished all these years. There had certainly been times when it sustained her. In spite of everything, even in spite of someone as wonderful as Rodney Whitehead coming into her life, that hope remained, the hope that one day her husband would return to her. She often sat and imagined that it had happened, and that they were happy now, contented with each other. It wasn't hard to imagine, even though she was thinking of something that had never been.

Now, standing there in the kitchen, she tried to tell herself Charlie would never be back to stay. It was obvious, after all, and she should face facts. That was surely better than clinging to a forlorn hope. But oddly, she couldn't convince herself, in spite of all the evidence.

She heard a tap on the door. She went through and stood with her ear to the panelling. 'Is that you, Charlie?'

'Yeah. Let us in, girl. It's freezin' out here.'

Dot opened the door and Charlie came in past her briskly. He went straight to the living room where he dropped his suitcase on the couch and then warmed his hands by the fire.

'I wouldn't want to be a brass ape in this weather,' he told Dot as she came in from the hallway.

'Pardon?'

'Nothin'. It's just an expression.' Charlie sat down, still rubbing his hands together near the coals.

'I see you got your things, then,' Dot said.

'Yeah. Didn't take long to pack. I seem to have less an' less every time I come to makin' a move.' The bag in fact contained new clothes, none of them more than a month old. They had been bought for him by Lynn, who'd said his wardrobe needed brightening up.

'You should be wearin' an overcoat on a night like this,' Dot observed.

'Haven't got one, love.' Charlie looked round the room, as if he were checking for changes. 'Your friend call, did he?'

'Yes, as a matter of fact he did.' Dot sat down awkwardly in the chair opposite Charlie's. 'He's not long gone, as a matter of fact.'

'Whoops,' Charlie said. 'That might have been awkward – if I'd turned up a bit earlier, I mean.' He grinned, emphasizing that he was making a light joke. 'Have a nice evenin', did you?'

'Very nice, yes.'

Charlie sat back and crossed his legs. 'How did you meet him?'

Dot shrugged. 'He gave a sermon at the chapel – he's a lay preacher. Afterwards I talked to him. He said any time I wanted to talk things over, I should give him a ring. It began like that. I went to see him, then one night he came to see me. We talked about religious things, an' the things we've got in common – both livin' on our own without partners, things like that. Nowadays it's a regular event, meetin' an talkin'.'

She had left out any reference to what Rodney had

132

said on her first visit to his house. He had confessed he was delighted she had got in touch. He sensed a kindred spirit, he told her. He wanted them to be friends. Dot knew he liked her very much; a woman could tell things like that straight away. They had agreed, though, that since they were both married, and since neither of them believed in divorce, their relationship would be purely platonic.

'Well, I suppose you're company for each other,' Charlie said.

'We certainly are. It's a blessin', havin' a friend.' She smiled, finding it easier now to talk about Rodney. 'He's even givin' Nick an' me Christmas dinner tomorrow.'

The little smile left Charlie's face. 'Really.' He sniffed. 'He's certainly takin' this friendship business seriously, isn't he?'

'That's the kind of man he is, Charlie.'

'Yeah.'

Charlie stared at the fire, wondering why he felt so edgy all of a sudden. She was free to do what she wanted, after all. And he had more than one edge on her. She didn't know it, but he often fell back on living with Dot's very own sister, Rose. As coincidences went it had been a beauty – although it had been mostly down to Charlie hanging around the old neighbourhood a few years before. There were enough similarities between Dot and Rose to make him feel nostalgic about his early days, and Rose was a pushover when it came to letting him have his way. She was no meal-ticket, though, and for the present she was out of bounds, due to a bad fight they'd had. Which didn't matter at all, he reflected now. He was on to a good thing, a better thing. So, taking all that into consideration, why did he feel so edgy about Dot having a man friend?

'Who is he anyway, this man? From round here, is he?'

'Oh, yes. He's in business. Quite well-to-do, as a matter of fact . . .'

Charlie listened, nodding, trying not to show his mounting resentment.

13

On Boxing Day afternoon, zipped up snugly in his new jerkin, Nick Cotton went out to play. Among the Christmas presents he'd had from his mother was a bow with six sucker-tipped arrows. He had taken it out with him, promising Dot that he wouldn't use it anywhere near windows or old people. For ten minutes he played at the end of the road, firing his little suckers on to a billboard, watching the house sidelong until the curtain finally stopped twitching. He found, generally, that if he played innocently for a few minutes, Dot relaxed her vigilance.

He gathered up his arrows and tucked them down the front of his jerkin, glancing along at the house one more time, then took off for Leighton Street at a trot, the bow swinging at his side.

He found Jackie Troughton without any trouble. Insofar as he was capable of liking anyone, Nick liked Jackie. Dot, though, had issued a lot of warnings about the lad. She believed, largely on instinct, that he was the worst of all the boys she'd forbidden Nick to play with. Jackie was big for his age, a year older than Nick and every bit as surly. Together they had pioneered a style of energetic vandalism that had caught on so strongly with other boys that, for a time, special two-man police patrols were posted around the district, trying to find the delinquents who regularly smashed windows, broke up displays outside shops and set fire to dustbins. Time and again Jackie reminded Nick and the other kids of the golden immunity conferred by the tenderness of their years. It was a slogan repeated many a time as little lads gleefully cut down washing lines, tore up vegetable patches and drew six-inch nails along car doors – 'They can't touch us for it.'

Squatting by an old brick coal-shed, Nick and Jackie compared notes about Christmas. They agreed it had been boring, and the presents this year had been duff. The best thing Jackie had been given, he said, was a penknife, but his dad had already confiscated it because Jackie had tested the sharpness of its blade on the edge of the kitchen table. Nick displayed the bow and arrows. Jackie didn't reckon they were up to much.

'They'd be better if you'd still got your knife,' Nick said.

When Jackie caught on, he decided it was worthwhile running the risk of pinching one of his mother's vegetable knives. There turned out to be no risk at all; Jackie's parents were watching television in the living room when he sneaked into the house by the back door. Ten minutes later, Nick possessed a bow and six wickedly sharp little arrows.

As the two lads were setting off to test the potential of the new weapons, Charlie Cotton was half a mile away in The Rumbold, leaning on the corner of the bar as he sullenly downed his sixth pint. He was swirling the dregs as Lynn walked in. She looked around for a moment, saw him and came across. She took in his rumpled appearance a piece at a time, clicking her tongue softly.

'You look terrible, Charlie.'

He turned his reddened eyes to her. 'I feel like death.'

'You shouldn't have had so much to drink.'

'I've only had a few pints.'

'Yesterday, I mean. I imagine that's what you were doin', wasn't it? Eatin' too much an' drinkin'.'

'Nah.' Charlie looked around, still wary of being seen talking in public to the wife of Sid the butcher. 'Want to sit down?'

'I'm easy.'

Charlie pointed to a table in the gloomiest corner of the bar. 'Take a chair. I'll bring you a drink.'

'Make it a Coke. I'd a bit too much myself yesterday.'

They settled into the shadows with their drinks. Charlie lit two cigarettes and passed one to Lynn. 'I reckon it's 'flu I've got,' he said.

'You shouldn't have come out, then.'

'Don't be daft. I said I'd meet you an' I'm a man of my word.' Charlie took a gulp of beer and shuddered. 'It's either 'flu, or I'm sufferin' from exposure. I'll most likely end up with piggin' pneumonia.'

'Exposure? How come?'

'The mate I'm stayin' with – he an' his missus went out for the day yesterday, visitin' relatives or somethin'. They went out while I was havin' a quick one down the local, an' they forgot to leave me a key.'

'Bloody hell. Do you mean you were locked out all day?'

'All day, yeah. Till half-ten last night.'

'An' you got no Christmas dinner or nothin'?'

'Bugger all.'

Lynn looked staggered. 'That's some mate you've got there.'

'I thought it was all a bit inconsiderate, I must say.'

Dot had no spare key, but Charlie had said he would be back before she left, so that he could stay in the house while she was out. He'd added that if he met an acquaintance in the pub who happened to invite him home to dinner, he wouldn't bother to come back. Dot prepared a meal for him to heat up, in case he was out of luck at the pub. He was out of luck at the pub. He got back to Dot's house, after drinking himself numb, to find the place locked up.

'Have you any idea,' Charlie asked Lynn, 'how hard it is to find somewhere out of the cold on Christmas Day?'

Lynn patted his hand. 'You poor love.'

'I kept on the move all afternoon an' the early part of the evenin', just so my blood didn't congeal. Then I had to walk into the next borough to find a pub open. I tell you, I was gettin' so desperate I nearly came round to Liz's place.'

Lynn shook her head sharply. 'That would have been a bad move. I told you already, that old man of hers don't hold with what I'm doin'. I didn't have as cold a Christmas Day as you had, but it was a stiff one. He kept droppin' remarks about it bein' people's place to be with their own families at Christmas, an' stuff about loyalty an' trustworthiness an' the meanin' of marriage. All of it quite jovial an' all said to Liz, mind you, but it was obviously aimed at me. He makes a better bitch than most women I've met.'

Charlie made a pained, sympathetic face. 'Never mind, love. We'll soon be fixed up on our own.'

'I hope so.' Lynn drew a squiggle in the beer puddle by her glass and gazed at it thoughtfully. 'Heard of any flats goin' yet?'

'Not yet,' Charlie said. 'It's a bit soon really, isn't it? I'll be able to turn up somethin' later on in the week, I fancy.'

'I can hardly wait.' Lynn put her hand on Charlie's knee and let it slide along his thigh. She winked at him. 'When we get a place we'll shut ourselves in an' not come out for the first three days, eh?'

'You bet.'

They fell silent, examining their private vistas as the pub's post-Christmas trade sluggishly came and went. Eventually Charlie looked at Lynn and said, 'How do you feel about it all now, then?'

'Leavin' Sid, you mean?'

Charlie nodded. 'An' havin' the prospect of settin' up house with me.'

'I feel different about it now,' Lynn said.

'Different?' Charlie's voice carried a tiny note of concern.

'Yeah.' Lynn pursed her glossy lips, trying to find a way to express herself clearly. 'Before, when we first decided on it, I was dead excited. The anticipation an' all that, you know?'

Charlie made the shadow of a nod.

'Now, well, Sid's behind me, as you might say. So the edge is off things. I mean the risky bit's over, the bit that took guts. From here on it's goin' to be easy.'

'But not excitin',' Charlie said.

Lynn looked perplexed now. 'That's not what I mean, no . . .'

'That's what it sounds like,' Charlie said huffily. He stood up and pushed back his chair. 'Excuse me, I'm goin' to get myself a scotch.'

At the bar, perhaps because he'd spent Christmas Day feeling thoroughly miserable, or maybe because he was miffed to discover that none of his old cronies wanted to know him any more, Charlie felt a deep wave of concern. It had been a long time since he had believed himself to be so open to disaster. His life over the past few years had seen some very low points, but there had always been something to hang on to, some angle that could be used to pull him out of whatever fix or doldrum he was in. Yesterday, seeing his friends snub him in the pub, finding a locked door at Dot's, roaming the length and breadth of Walford without finding a spark of warmth, he had felt a very keen despair. It had been the effect of the cold, of course, and the hunger, and the weariness. But it proved to him that he *wasn't* protected by any special streak of luck, or by anything else. All he'd had to hold on to, by the time it turned dark, was the thought that Lynn was there. She was his. She was the only creature in a bleak world that cared a toss for him.

Now he was beginning to worry about her. She was

wavering, he could feel it. Maybe she didn't feel it yet, not properly, but Charlie did. He knew the early cooling signs in a woman. What had looked so great to her in prospect wasn't so rosy now it was turning to reality. She was getting the first twinges of what would be misgivings, then there would be real doubt, then –

'Christ!'

A man beside him at the bar turned and looked. Charlie realized he had said it aloud. It had slipped out on the tide of a small panic. *If he lost Lynn he lost everything!* He thought of all that security being snatched from his grasp. Gulping, he paid for his drink and turned back to the table, putting on an apologetic smile.

'Sorry, love,' he said as he sat down. 'I'm a bit touchy. It's because I'm feelin' so rotten.'

'I understand,' Lynn said.

Charlie examined her smile. Was it as warm as it used to be? Was it as eager?

'Drink your scotch an' you'll feel better.'

'Yeah.' He took a gulp and let it burn its way to his stomach. 'Listen,' he said. 'You an' me – the arrangement's still OK, isn't it? I mean I don't want you goin' into anythin' you might think you'll regret. That wouldn't be fair on you.'

'Charlie, nothin's changed. It's only the way I look at it that's different. I still want us to have our own place an' live there together. Straight up.'

'Yeah, of course. Sorry. I'm just . . .' He spiralled his hand over his head. 'Ignore me.'

'Dopey,' Lynn said. She stuck her tongue out at him and giggled. 'You'll feel brighter when you've located a flat for us. The whole trouble is that nothin's properly settled yet.'

'Sure,' Charlie said.

Nothing was settled, he thought. That was truer than she thought. The set-up was turning sour on him, it was a feeling he couldn't shake. He looked up from his glass. Lynn was still smiling at him. He tried to smile back.

Dot moved away from the open door and let Inspector Cuthbert come in. He had said nothing when she opened the door. All he had done was indicate, with one gloved hand, that he wanted to come into the house. Dot closed the door again as he stepped into the living room. When she joined him he was standing with his back to the fireplace. His face was stern.

'Is it – '

'Yes, it's your son,' the inspector snapped. 'Again.'

Dot's fingers tented in a trembling gesture of prayer. 'What's happened?'

'He's committed another crime, of course. Two crimes, in fact. You didn't think I'd arrived to deliver a certificate of commendation, did you?'

'But he was only playin' out on the street,' Dot wailed, clutching the sideboard for support.

'What he did, Mrs Cotton, does not come under the category of play.'

Dot moved gingerly away from the sideboard and eased herself on to the arm of the sofa. She had turned white and her lips were trembling. 'You're sure it was him? I mean it seems a bit unlikely to me . . .'

'If it seems unlikely, then you're not facing facts. You've been told, by someone who knows, that your boy has a disturbed personality. A child he may be, but he's got the instincts of a monster.' Inspector Cuthbert folded his arms and spread his feet, an instinctive gesture of authority which made Dot inch backwards. 'You were warned that he should be watched. At all times. The people at his school were warned too. He's *that* bad. There's a few like him around here. Maybe it's the environment, Mrs Cotton, or something that happened to them when they were smaller. Frankly, I don't believe any of the namby-pamby liberal explanations for them being the way they are. They're rotten little people, born that way, and they'll likely be rotten for the rest of their lives. When they're older it'll be the job of people like me to protect the rest of the community from them. For now, though, you're supposed to do that.'

'But how can I?' Dot squeaked. 'I can't stand over him every hour of the day, I can't – '

'I don't care how you do it. But I think you should have taken the warnings seriously and made more of an effort. I'll tell you this – as of today, your hopes of even trying to control the boy have turned very slim.'

Dot put her head on one side, trying to take that in.

'What I'm saying, Mrs Cotton, is that I'm going to press to have your Nick put away.'

'You can't do that!'

'He's a menace. You can't control him. He's got no father to control him. So the authorities'll have to do something. There's steps they can take, in exceptional cases. And this is an exceptional case if ever I saw one. My report's going to say so, in the strongest terms.'

'They don't put kids in prison!'

The inspector nodded sharply. 'That's right, they don't. There's another name for where they put them – but the important thing is they're *put* somewhere. People are protected from them.'

Dot was beyond tears. The fear of losing Nick had brought her to her feet again, eyes wide, hands clenched, trying to form a barrier to the inspector's intent. 'What can he have done that's so terrible? He's so small you can pick him up – he's not a danger to anybody.'

'You know better than that,' Cuthbert sighed. 'You can pick up any amount of small things that could kill you. For your information, your son and another boy waylaid two young girls on Catmore Road and took their money off them. The girls were then allowed to go, but as they went your son took it into his head to fire wooden arrows at them from a plastic bow.'

'That's just a toy!'

'Not now, it isn't. Your Nick had a pocketful of rubber suckers on him when he was picked up. He probably couldn't wait to pull them off and sharpen the arrows. The upshot, Mrs Cotton, is that one girl has a nasty wound under her eye. It needed stitches. She got it when she stopped and turned, wondering what had made the other wound on the back of her leg.'

Dot clenched her teeth, clamping back a moan.

'Nick will be brought back home later today,' the inspector said. 'See to it that he stays in. In a couple of days we'll be able to let you know what's to be done with him.' He moved to the door then stopped. He examined the shiny toes of his shoes for a moment. 'I didn't need to come and tell you all this,' he said. 'I could have sent a constable. But I wanted to let you know how I feel – I'm a self-indulgent man, you see. I want you to know that, in my estimation, your son is going to grow into a particularly nasty villain. I don't see how that can be stopped.'

Dot's eyes were pleading for him to say no more.

'What I want you to know, most of all,' the inspector went on, 'is that although I'm sorry for you, I still believe you've let him get as bad as he is. He's only eighty-odd months old, but already the badness has set in him. There's bound to be *some* neglect underlying that fact.'

'Nick's never been neglected!'

'You've neglected to discipline him. You've never put up barriers, and kids need barriers, otherwise they don't know there are such things as boundaries.' The inspector turned and stepped into the passage. 'For your own good be harder with him, for as long as he's your responsibility. It might be too late, but anything's worth a try.'

For minutes after the inspector had gone, Dot stood in

the middle of the living room, feeling every frailty in her merge to a terrible emptiness. She felt helpless, useless, lost. Every effort she had expended in life had been for nothing – with her son, her marriage, everything. She was scarcely adequate to sustain her own personality. How could the inspector know that hard as she tried, she had no effect on anything?

She grasped the edge of the table and lowered herself to her knees. With hands clasped and head bowed she prayed, her voice trembling. 'Hear me God my saviour and bring peace to my troubled heart. Grant me strength . . .'

14

Two days before New Year's Eve Charlie and Lynn made a tour of the newsagents', grocers' and tobacconists' windows along the High Road. They were looking for advertisements of flats to rent. Contrary to what Charlie had said at the outset, there weren't plenty of places available. There were bedsitters for single occupancy, offers to share apartments and houses, and there were flats and houses for sale; but no flats to rent.

'Some bloody place this is,' Lynn muttered as they finished scanning the tenth set of advertisement cards on their route. Her temper had been deteriorating steadily as they tramped the cold pavements. 'In Islington there's more places than you can count.'

'But we can't live in Islington,' Charlie pointed out.

'I can't live in flamin' Walford any longer. I'll tell you that. I'm pig sick of it. Stayin' at Liz's is like bein' in prison.'

Charlie stuck a cigarette in his mouth and shielded the match with his hand. He took a deep puff and looked up and down the road. 'I don't know what to do next, love.'

'Huh.' Lynn drew her fur jacket closer about her. 'An' you're the guy that was goin' to fix everythin' up.'

'I can't do the impossible, Lynn. Be fair.' Since his feelings of insecurity had set in, he'd tended to adopt a doggish downcast look every time Lynn got displeased about anything. 'I don't like the situation any better than you do, but like I say, I'm not up to doin' what's impossible.'

'Then do what's possible, for God's sake. How can you say it's impossible to find a poxy two room flat in a borough the size of this? Ain't you got any contacts? Don't you know *anybody* that can help?'

'If I did, I'd be straight on to them . . .'

'Christ.' Lynn jerked her collar up, obscuring half of her face. 'You're useless, do you know that?'

'Aw, come on, love.' Charlie put his hand on her shoulder. 'You're lettin' yourself get upset about nothin'.'

'Nothin'?' Lynn shrugged his hand away. 'Havin' nowhere to live is *nothin'*, is it? It might be nothin' if you've dossed around most of your days, but I'm used to better than that.'

Charlie stared helplessly across the road. This was it, he thought. It was about to happen and he was powerless to stop it. She was going to walk out on him and cancel everything. Disaster was staring him right in the face. *He had to do something*. The more that became a certainty, the more helpless he felt.

'We could try an agency,' he said feebly. 'I know you don't like the idea, but I reckon it's our only hope.'

'No chance,' Lynn snapped. 'They want references, for a start, an' they always check up on them. Even if I *could* tell them my last address an' all the rest of it, it'd take a couple of weeks for the deal to go through. On top of that, they usually want key money an' three months' rent in advance. I'm not throwin' my money away like that – not even if they could get us a place right this bloody minute.'

Charlie felt a taut barrier go up between them. He tried to hurdle it. 'Money's not everythin', love. I really think we should try an agency. I can get some references sorted out. There's ways of doin' these things.' He was improvising now. All he wanted to do was bring her close to him again. Details could be attended to later. 'What's a few quid if it gets us out of a hole?'

Lynn turned and faced him squarely. Her cosmetically

146

tanned features had stiffened. 'I just love the way you talk about my money as if it was yours.'

Charlie stared innocently. 'What do you mean?'

'I mean just what I say.' Her eyes narrowed a fraction. 'While I'm on the subject – do you realize you've spent more of my money these last six days than I have? How much of that fifty's left?'

Charlie frowned, pretending to calculate. 'Dunno. A few quid, I suppose. I've had rent to pay, an' there's the meals an' drinks we've had . . .'

'I paid for the meals an' half the drinks,' Lynn said. 'I caught a flash of the dregs when we were in the pub last night. There's no more than three quid left.'

'Ah, but wait . . .' Charlie conjured a rapid explanation. 'I don't carry it all with me. God, no. I've maybe twenty-five still at my digs.'

Lynn made a sour face, rejecting the story.

'That's straight, love. I swear it. I'm not daft enough to carry the whole caboodle about with me.'

'Jesus wept . . .' Lynn wasn't looking at Charlie any more. She was staring past his shoulder at the road.

Charlie turned. He saw people and traffic, nothing special. 'What? What is it?'

A green Jaguar drew in sharply at the kerb. The driver got out and slammed his door.

'Oh buggery,' Charlie breathed.

It was Sid the butcher. He was striding round the car towards them, buttoned up in a camel coat that emphasized his muscular bulk. His red, thick-featured face was a churning mixture of triumph and anger.

'You!' he barked, pointing at Charlie. 'Stay right where you are!' He stepped close to Lynn, his mouth pursing as if he were going to spit in her face. She backed away and he grabbed her arm. 'Get in the car!'

'Sod off!'

'Get in or I'll belt you right here on the street!' Sid

swung himself in a half circle, throwing Lynn against the side of the car.

'I'll scream for the cops if you don't let me go!'

'Get *in*, you cowin' bitch!'

The fight drained from Lynn as Sid balled his fist at her. She glanced at Charlie, standing stoop-shouldered and white behind Sid, then she jerked open the front passenger door and slid into the car. Sid pushed the door shut and turned to Charlie. 'Right, shitface.' He looked along the pavement and pointed. 'Over there, at the side of that shop. Move.'

'Look, mate, you're gettin' this all wrong . . .' Charlie's mouth was so dry he could hardly speak. 'None of this has anythin' to do with me – '

'Move!'

Somehow Charlie put the movements together and made his legs take him to the narrow alley. Sid walked close behind him. In the car Lynn stared straight ahead, seeing nothing, her face gaunt.

When they cleared the street Sid spread the fingers of one hand and pushed Charlie hard between the shoulder blades. He grunted as his chest slammed against the wall.

'Now turn an' face me.'

Charlie turned slowly, tensing himself. He pressed his back against the bricks. 'Please, I'm – ' He swallowed hard, getting a flashing memory of the time on Oxford Street and later in the club, the big man staring at him, meaning him harm. 'I'm not the bloke you're after, honest – '

'You're Charlie Cotton,' Sid growled, 'the bloke – or should I say the sneakin', connivin' heap of crap – that I'm after.' He pushed his face close. 'That I've *got*.' He grasped Charlie's lapels and twisted them, taking a tight grip. 'What made you think you'd get away with it, eh?'

'Look, I'm beggin' you – '

'Did you really think I wouldn't find her? All I had to

do was check round her crummy mates. Anythin' that cow gets up to, one or other of her mates knows about it. An' I can always make them talk.' Sid drew his head back, studying Charlie's face. 'She's had a few flings, but you're the only one she's ever run away with. What's special about you? Eh?'

Cold as it was, Charlie was sweating. 'I'm nothin' special, mate – '

'Don't bleedin' call me mate.'

'Sorry. I – '

'Shut it. Listen instead. You shit on me, so you're gettin' what you deserve. It's justice. I just want you to know that. You're gettin' nothin' you didn't work for.'

Paralysed, Charlie watched Sid's big head move back further still. The grip on his lapels got tighter.

'Bastard!' Sid snarled. He hunched suddenly and smashed his forehead on Charlie's nose. Charlie howled, staggered as Sid released him, then fell. Sid kicked him on the chest, then twice in the groin. As Charlie rolled over the boot landed on his kidney. He didn't feel it. He had passed out after the first kick in the groin.

When the light came back, and all the pain with it, he was lying in a hospital bed. A prissy-faced middle-aged nurse was bending over him.

'Can you hear me?'

Charlie nodded. Pain sliced across his face.

'Do you remember what happened?'

He tried. It came back in a rush. He nodded again, more carefully this time.

'A policeman will be taking details later, when you're feeling better. Have you any relatives we can get in touch with?'

Charlie thought about it. He could easily get Dot to look after him. He'd need looking after. Then he remembered her friend. Mr Goody-Goody the chemist. Whitehead. The interloper. Beneath his pain Charlie felt

149

resentment flooding again. It had happened, he was right out in the cold with nothing, nobody. He looked at the nurse and shook his head.

'Are you sure?'

'Sure,' he croaked.

'I'll be back shortly. Just lie there and rest.'

Charlie watched her go. What else did she think he could do but lie there and rest? His head and back throbbed, it felt like there was a sharp-edged weight on his chest, and there was an ominous hot numbness between his legs. It had happened all over again. He had broken some rules and he'd been given a hammering. At an estimate, he reckoned he'd been hurt just as badly as he had the first time.

Except this time he couldn't go to Dot. That was the big difference. History wasn't quite repeating itself. She was his legal wife, but he couldn't go to her. Who the hell else could he go to? Resentment danced on the perimeter of his pain. Between that first hammering and this one a lot had happened. And Dot had come out of those years a lot better than old Charlie Cotton. She had prospects. He had none.

He thought of Sid's snarling face and suddenly he wanted to hurt back. He couldn't hurt Sid. But he wanted to hurt. He didn't want to go down without punching out and causing a bit of damage on his own account.

For a few more minutes Charlie lay there thinking and hurting. Then he reached a soothing decision and stopped thinking.

The following afternoon Dot visited her doctor. Since he had told her she was neuraesthenic she had embraced the new condition with the fervour of a convert. Like her faith, her new ailment had to be suffered for. The latest symptom was bouts of itching on both arms and across her shoulders.

'You're bringing it on yourself,' Dr Lewis told her.

'How can I be doing that?'

'Automatically.' Lewis was nearing retirement. His patience with the likes of Dot had gone years ago. He sat back in his swivel chair and scratched his bald head. 'You're so good at automatic symptom creation, Mrs Cotton, that I fancy you could turn yourself black, if your nervous system put its mind to it.'

Dot wasn't sure if he was joking. He never smiled, so she could never tell. 'What am I to do about it then, Doctor?'

'I'll give you a prescription for some tablets. They'll stop the itching, but I'll warn you now, they might make you terribly thirsty.' Dr Lewis drew his pad towards him and scribbled out the name of a placebo. He found that medicines which did absolutely nothing tended to work with Dot, so long as he warned her that they would cause some other tedious symptom. 'There you are.'

'Thanks.' Dot folded the slip and put it in her handbag.

'Are you eating any better?' Lewis asked her. 'Or are you still living on milky tea and cigarettes?'

'I have my regular meals.'

'Sausage rolls and cakes aren't meals. Have you been getting some vegetables inside you, like I said you should?'

Dot made a face. 'I've never liked vegetables, Doctor.'

Lewis sighed. 'Well, one way or another, feed yourself up. You're underweight and that helps nothing.'

'I'll do that.' Dot stood up and went to the door. Having been given another prescription, which was all she wanted, she was anxious to leave. Nick was with a neighbour, but even so she was worried in case he found some way to talk the woman round and get out to play. 'Thanks very much for the tablets.'

She took the prescription to Rodney Whitehead's

chemist's shop. He was behind the counter in his white coat, giving an old lady her change.

'My sister's ever so grateful for that ointment you sold her,' the customer was saying. 'She tells everybody what a miracle worker you are.'

Rodney shook his head. 'I dressed her wounds,' he said, 'God healed her.'

The old woman nodded, smiling uncertainly, and left.

Rodney came along the counter to Dot. 'How are you today?' he asked solicitously. At their last meeting she'd had a touch of migraine.

'Much better, thanks.' She handed over the prescription. 'The doctor thinks I should have these.'

Rodney put down the prescription without looking at it. 'Instead of you having to wait, why don't you let me drop the prescription off when I'm on my way home?'

'Oh, would you? That'd be lovely. I'm in a bit of a rush, anyway.'

'It's no trouble at all, Dot.'

When she had gone Rodney served another customer, then asked another if he would mind waiting, because the telephone was ringing.

'Whitehead Chemists,' he murmured into the mouth-piece. 'Rodney Whitehead speaking. Can I help you?'

There was a pause at the other end of the line, then a throaty, rather breathless voice said, 'It's me that can help you. To avoid a bit of trouble, that is.'

Rodney frowned delicately. 'I beg your pardon?'

'You're friendly with a Mrs Dot Cotton, right? You visit her an' that.'

The frown deepened. 'I see the lady occasionally, yes.'

'Well my advice is, don't see her any more.'

Rodney moistened his lips. 'Who is this speaking?'

Another pause and some more laboured breathing, then the voice said, 'It's somebody that'll do you an' your business a lot of harm if you don't follow the advice.'

Appalled, Rodney stared across the shop at a row of coloured bottles. 'Just what do you mean by harm?'

The man on the other end of the line took less than a minute to tell him. Within half that time Rodney turned very pale. He put down the receiver as the line went dead.

The man waiting to be served was staring at him. 'Are you all right, mate?'

Rodney didn't reply. Feeling behind him, he drew forward a little stool. He sat down and buried his face in his hands.

15

'Nick's goin' before a Board,' Dot told her neighbour, Mrs Ratcliffe. 'I don't know what it's about, the Board I mean, but they want to hear the social people's report on him, an' the remedial woman's – the child psychologist's an' all.'

'That's an awful lot of reports for such a little lad.' Mrs Ratcliffe sipped her tea and leaned an elbow on Dot's kitchen drainer. Dot had invited her in on an impulse. It usually made her nervous to have other women in the house; she always felt they'd start to criticize the way she did things. 'What do they reckon's up with him, anyway?'

'I've no idea. If you ask me, it's a lot of nonsense. I've heard that highly intelligent children are always a problem when they're younger – it's somethin' to do with their brain cells havin' to hold all that cleverness. Nick's just a very bright boy who's goin' through a normal phase.'

'What's he supposed to have done that's made all them people make out reports on him, then?' Mrs Ratcliffe asked.

'Oh, just mischief. Little things. A kiddie doesn't have to do much nowadays to have the authorities after him. I fancy them specialists just like to show off their knowledge to one another.'

It was unusual for Dot to discuss Nick with anyone. This morning she felt she had to talk, though. She envied the Catholics with their confessionals. If she was a Catholic, she often thought, she'd never be out of that little box. The next best thing to the secrecy of the confessional, though, was Mrs Ratcliffe. Like Dot, she never mixed much with the other neighbours. She was a widow, and since her husband had died four years ago she hardly ever went out. 'When George was here he gave me a bit of purpose,' she'd once told Dot as they talked over the back fence. 'Now every day's like a loose end.' Talking to Mrs Ratcliffe was a process that ended right there. She never transmitted gossip, and she had a terrible memory, anyway.

'I don't have no truck with the authorities, Mrs Cotton. George always said that once they got a foot in your life, they forced their way in an' never gave you no peace ever after.'

'He was right,' Dot sighed. She wasn't sure if talking to Mrs Ratcliffe was helping. The panicky sensations were still with her. They came in waves, and she could feel another one coming now. 'More tea?' she said, twitching the teapot on its heatproof mat. 'I always say it takes two cups before it does you any good.'

'No thanks.' Mrs Ratcliffe put down her cup. 'I've got to get back.' She smiled apologetically, looking slightly embarrassed. 'The cat, you see. He has to be fed dead on eleven. Then there's my programme at a quarter past, on the wireless. I never miss it. I often get the feeling that somethin' terrible would happen if I ever did miss it.'

Dot saw her to the door and said cheerio. As she went back to the kitchen she reflected that there were similarities between herself and Mrs Ratcliffe, if what she'd said about the radio programme was anything to go by.

She poured herself another cup of tea, spooned in the sugar and topped up the cup with milk. She could hear Nick through in his room, banging at something metallic. He'd told her he was making a ray machine, whatever that was. Something he'd seen in a comic, she supposed.

'Oh, Lord.' Dot put a hand to her forehead. Today she simply couldn't think straight for more than a minute at a time. She had panics, shivers, her head ached and the itching had shifted to her legs. She wondered if she should take another couple of the tablets.

She looked at the bottle on the shelf. Just seeing it brought on a helpless need to cry. The tablets had been dropped through the letterbox the evening before. The bottle had been in an envelope with Rodney Whitehead's name printed on it. There had been a note in the envelope, too. Taking a deep breath to settle herself, Dot pulled the crumpled paper from her apron pocket and read it for maybe the twentieth time.

> Dot,
> *It is painful for me to write this, so I will make it brief. I have to tell you that I can no longer visit you, or in any way behave like a friend to you. Please do not be offended, for I still think highly of you. I always will. But for very personal reasons our relationship, which gave me so much pleasure, must now be ended.*
> > *Yours*
> > *Rodney*

Dot had puzzled over the note, ached over it, and spent most of a sleepless night trying to understand why the most comforting feature of her life had been wiped out. Perhaps Rodney's wife had come back to him. That was the possibility Dot clung to, since she couldn't think of another one. It gave her no comfort, though. It merely kept the hurt, which felt like a grief, at a bearable level.

And then there was Charlie. He hadn't come back last night. She wondered for a while if he had just left without warning, as he had done before. But then she remembered his things. He hadn't taken them. So perhaps he had stayed at a friend's place. That was another possibility Dot tried to hold to; the other one, that he had been run over, was too terrible to contemplate.

She took her tea into the living room, wishing something would happen, anything at all, just to distract her from herself. At a time like this she would even prefer a row with her mother to the throbbing inertia that enclosed her. But she hadn't seen her mother since Nick was a baby. Martha had moved away, and she had never given Dot her address. That was another rejection. Everybody seemed to move out on her, Dot thought bleakly.

There was a knock at the door. Dot jumped so violently she spilled tea on her fingers. She put the cup on the table and hurried to the door, mopping her hand on her apron. It could be Rodney, come to say sorry, forget the note . . .

She pulled open the door and saw Charlie there. For a moment she wasn't too sure it was him at all. His face was bruised and blotchy and he stood as if he was carrying something heavy on his back.

'Hello, love,' he said, coming in past her. Dot noticed he was limping.

She followed him into the living room. 'What happened to you?'

'Bit of an accident,' Charlie said, easing down on to the couch. 'Had to go to hospital overnight.'

'Were you run over, or what?'

'Nah, I was takin' one of the old shortcuts, goin' over a fence. I lost my balance and wallop, landed in a pile of rocks. I got myself to the hospital an' they kept me in.'

'They should have let me know,' Dot said, heading for the kitchen to put on the kettle.

'I asked them not to, love. Didn't want to impose on you, get you upset an' that.'

When Dot had made more tea she sat on the edge of an armchair, sipping and listening as Charlie explained his new predicament.

'I was supposed to start my new job in the New Year. But I can't, not in this condition. They told me at the hospital I have to take it easy for a couple of weeks, at least. My big problem is, because I'm not earnin' I can't afford digs. I've got to find somewhere, though. I can't spend much time out of doors in this weather.' Charlie sighed. 'I'm only grateful I've got the use of this sofa at night.'

'But you can stay here, Charlie,' Dot said.

He looked at her. 'But what about your friend? You said before it would make things awkward, me bein' here.' As Dot began to say something he put up a hand. 'No, I won't hear of it. You've got your private life to lead. I'm not goin' to do anythin' to interfere with that. It's out of the question.'

'Charlie, listen.' Dot stood up, gesturing animatedly, trying to make him see he was welcome. 'There's no problem any more. You can stay here. I'd like you to.'

'I don't get it.'

'I'm not goin' to be seein' Rodney any more. I won't go into the details, but that's the way things are. You wouldn't be in the way. Honestly.'

Charlie made a show of reluctance. 'Well, if you're sure. I mean you're not just sayin' that, are you? You're not deliberately puttin' a strain on your friendship with whatsisname, just to ease things for me?'

'Of course I'm not. You can stay here an' I can feed you an' look after you for a bit. Sit tight an' I'll get you some more tea.'

In the kitchen, her hands trembling as she filled the kettle, Dot felt a wonderful surge of relief. It was as if a prayer had been answered. One door had closed and another had swung open, just like the proverb said. She was sorry Charlie had had his accident, of course. But there was providence in it. He would stay and she would care for him. He would see what a good wife she could be, and he would learn that her companionship was true and fulfilling. It was what she had dreamed about and hoped for.

When she had put the kettle on she went back to the

living room. 'Once I've given you your tea,' she told Charlie, 'I'll go out to the shops an' get you somethin' special for your tea tonight.'

Charlie smiled at her, looking pathetic with his bruises and swellings. 'You're an angel, Dot,' he said huskily. 'I don't deserve you.'

'Don't talk silly,' Dot murmured, turning back to the kitchen as the blush rose along her neck and flooded her cheeks.

The bright cold day passed to evening. There was ice in the air. In her living room Dot sat alone by the fire, still as an effigy. She could feel very little, beyond the fog of stillness around her.

If it weren't for hope, Rodney had said, the heart would break. The words came to Dot from nowhere, from the vacuum inside her. Thinking was difficult. It was patchwork with blanks between the patches. Hope. She didn't believe she had any now. She couldn't believe she ever would, again. She wasn't sure if her heart was breaking, or had already broken, or had simply shrivelled in her.

The memory came back, a recent memory that seemed old, because it had repeated itself so many times over the hours. She and Nick had come back from the shops with pork chops and some fruit. Dot had started telling Charlie what she'd brought before she got into the living room. She stopped talking abruptly when she discovered he wasn't there. The bathroom door was open, so he wasn't there, either. Nor in either of the bedrooms. Charlie wasn't in the house.

Then she noticed his suitcase had gone.

For half an hour she stood in the kitchen, drinking tea, wondering. When she went to the bedroom to get her migraine tablets she stopped wondering. The drawer on the bedside table was partly open. She never left drawers open. She couldn't sleep if she thought there was a drawer open somewhere in the house.

The tin box had gone. It was a sweet tin where she kept the money she'd been saving for two years. Money to get things Nick would need when he went to secondary school, and to use in an emergency. She thought of it as a nest egg. Twenty-eight pounds in notes and coins.

Now, sitting by the fire without feeling its warmth, Dot felt the first pang of hurt. She stood up, feeling she had to move or be sucked down into darkness. As she crossed the room she heard Nick make a sound in his sleep. It was a baby sound, full of softness.

Dot closed her eyes. She mustn't think, not now that it was becoming painfully easy. She must do something else. *Even in despair, hope casts down a lifeline.* Rodney had said that too, in one of his sermons. It had come unbidden. Dot held on to the words, hearing Nick make that little sound again. There was her hope, she decided. Her son would be her salvation.

She went to the room and looked at him. In the dim light from the passage he looked serene. His face was smooth with innocence.

'God bless you,' Dot whispered. She bent and kissed his cheek.

No matter what, she told herself, finding grim peace in the thought, she would shield that boy. She would live for him and him alone. He was God's gift to her. She would mould her solitary gift from roughness to perfection. All else that had seemed God-given had vanished, but Dot silently swore that through her boy, something worthwhile would come of her cold life.